Jane Eyre

First published in 2003 by Usborne Publishing Ltd,
Usborne House, 83-85 Saffron Hill,
London EC1N 8RT, England.
www.usborne.com

A catalogue record for this title is available
from the British Library.

ISBN 07945 06585

Printed in Great Britain

Designed by Sarah Cronin
Series editors: Jane Chisholm and Rosie Dickins
Series designer: Mary Cartwright
Cover photographs © Lassimo Listri/CORBIS and
Anna Palma/CORBIS
Cover design by Glen Bird
With thanks to Georgina Andrews

Jane Eyre

From the story by Charlotte Brontë

Retold by Anna Claybourne

Illustrated by Bob Harvey

Contents

Introduction

Ever since *Jane Eyre* was first published, in 1847, it has been one of the best-known and best-loved books in the English language. Its author, Charlotte Brontë, was to become extremely famous, but when *Jane Eyre* first appeared, she used a false male name, Currer Bell. This was because it was very difficult in those days for women to be taken seriously as writers — despite the success of earlier female novelists such as Jane Austen. By pretending to be a man, Charlotte Brontë gave her novel a much better chance of being accepted.

Charlotte was 31 when *Jane Eyre* was published, but she had been writing all her life. As children, she, her brother Branwell and her sisters Emily and Anne spent their time making up imaginary worlds and writing about them in tiny books, some of which survive to this day. Charlotte and Branwell invented an African kingdom called Angria, while Emily and Anne created a rival kingdom, Gondal. When the Brontë girls grew up, writing, along with teaching, was one of the few careers open to them, and Charlotte, Emily and Anne all became novelists.

Although they were very close to each other, life was hard for the Brontë children. They lived in Haworth, a moorland village in Yorkshire, in the north of England, and were the children of the local vicar. The family had moved there in 1820, but in 1821, when Charlotte was just five, her mother died of cancer. Her aunt, Elizabeth Branwell, came to look after her and her brother and sisters.

More tragedy was to follow. In 1824, the four oldest children, Elizabeth, Maria, Charlotte and Emily, were sent away to Cowan Bridge, a school for the daughters of clergymen. The following year, an epidemic of the deadly disease tuberculosis swept through the school, and Elizabeth and Maria fell ill. They were sent home, but both died. Charlotte and Emily were brought home too, and from then on Charlotte grew up as the oldest in the family.

Patrick Brontë, Charlotte's father, had been born into poverty in Ireland, but his intelligence and hard work had won him a place at Cambridge University, and he believed in a good education for both girls and boys. The parsonage was filled with books, including some that Patrick had written himself, and all his children loved to read.

But being so bookish made it hard for the Brontës to make friends with the other village children, whose parents were mainly farmers and factory workers. Charlotte often felt she was surrounded by people who did not understand her and were not as clever as her − a feeling which is reflected in the pages of *Jane Eyre*.

In fact, like Charlotte's other novels, *Jane Eyre* contains many elements and situations based on her own life. Lowood, the harsh, strict charity school Jane attends, is based on Charlotte's experiences at Cowan Bridge, and the character of Jane's friend Helen Burns is thought to be based on one of Charlotte's older sisters. When she was 19, Charlotte became a teacher at another school, Roe Head, and later went to work as a governess – experiences which were also recreated in *Jane Eyre*. And, like Jane, Charlotte despaired over her appearance, feeling that she was too small, thin and unattractive to find a husband. When she did finally fall head-over-heels in love, it was with a married man, and her feelings were not returned.

Charlotte and her sisters Emily and Anne planned to open a school of their own in Haworth. But first, in order to improve their skills, Charlotte and Emily went to Brussels to study languages while teaching English. There, Charlotte fell for a married professor named Monsieur Heger. After their aunt died, Emily came home to look after their father, but Charlotte stayed in Brussels for nearly two years. She became obsessed with Monsieur Heger, and although he was not interested in her, this love was to overshadow the rest of her life. Most of her novels depict lonely, shy heroines who fall in love with older men – though, of course, in her fiction Charlotte was free to make these love stories turn out however she wanted.

The school the sisters had planned was not a success, so instead they turned to their writing. All three of them had written poetry, and in 1846, they published a book of poems using the male names Currer, Ellis and Acton Bell. It didn't sell, but the sisters did not give up. The following year, *Wuthering Heights*, a novel by Ellis Bell (Emily Brontë), and *Agnes Grey*, by Acton Bell (Anne Brontë), were both accepted for publication. Several publishers turned down Charlotte's first novel, *The Professor*, but her second, *Jane Eyre*, was accepted immediately. By the end of 1847, all three novels were out, and the Bell brothers became a national sensation.

From the start, people wondered who the Bells were, and some thought they might be women. They were soon forced to come clean. *Jane Eyre* was by far the most popular of the three novels, and when Anne's second book, *The Tenant of Wildfell Hall*, came out, her publisher tried to pretend it was by Currer, not Acton, Bell. So Charlotte and Anne went to visit their publishers in London, and revealed for the first time who they really were.

Charlotte now began her life as a full-time writer, but tragedy was about to strike yet again. In the summer of 1848, her brother Branwell Brontë, who was an alcoholic and drug addict, became very ill. He died that September. As the autumn drew on, it turned out that Emily was ill too, probably with tuberculosis. She continued running the parsonage, refusing to see a doctor, and in December 1848, she too died, aged just 29.

To Charlotte's horror, Anne, her only remaining sibling, was also diagnosed with TB. She tried all kinds of medicines, and in May 1849 Charlotte went with her to the seaside town of Scarborough, as sea air was thought to help cure the disease. But Anne died there, leaving Charlotte heartbroken.

Over the next few years, Charlotte concentrated on her writing, and published two more novels, *Shirley* in 1849, and *Villette* – which some see as her best work – in 1853. She also visited London several times. There she met other famous authors, such as Mrs. Gaskell and William Thackeray, had her portrait painted, and became more and more famous.

Back in Haworth, the Reverend Arthur Bell Nicholls, a poor curate who worked with her father, proposed marriage to Charlotte in 1852. At first she said no, but she eventually married him in 1854.

Although she was not really in love with him, her new husband did bring Charlotte some comfort and happiness. But she was constantly depressed over the deaths of her siblings, and when she caught pneumonia the following year, she seemed to give up on life, even though her illness could have been treated. While pregnant with her first child, she died in March 1855, aged only 38.

After her death, Charlotte's first novel, *The Professor*, was finally published, and the novelist Mrs. Gaskell wrote a biography of her, describing her life. It helped to make the Brontë sisters as famous for their real lives as for their novels, and both have fascinated readers ever since.

The Red Room

There was no possibility of taking a walk that day. It was too gloomy, windy and wet. Instead, we had to amuse ourselves indoors. My cousins, Eliza, John and Georgiana Reed, were in the drawing room, gathered around their mother by the fireside, but I was not allowed to join the group.

"You, Jane, are excluded from our company until I hear from Bessie that you can behave like a proper, sweet little girl," Mrs. Reed had announced.

"What does Bessie say I have done?" I asked.

"Don't answer me back," she snapped. "Go and sit somewhere else until you can speak nicely."

Obeying her, I went into the breakfast-room. I took one of the books I loved best, *Bewick's History of British Birds*, from the bookcase, and climbed into the large window seat. I drew the curtain closed, sealing myself inside my own little space next to the window. As the wind and rain battered the glass, I immersed myself in another world. I loved to gaze at the seagull nestling on its rocky ledge, and the long-eared owl standing watch over a dark churchyard.

But my peace was soon shattered.

"Hey! Jane Eyre!" John Reed had come into the room. "Where has she gone? Eliza! Tell Mama! Jane's run away!"

"She's in the window seat, John, to be sure," came his sister's voice.

I pulled the heavy curtain aside, before he could drag me out. There he stood, bulky and brainless, with his flabby cheeks and ugly, sneering grin. John was fourteen, four years older than me, and he bullied and attacked me constantly. No one in the house ever stopped him – the servants didn't dare to upset him, and his mother wouldn't hear a word said against him. I hated and feared him with every bone in my body.

"Stop hiding behind curtains and sneaking about, you little rat," he said. Then he suddenly hit me hard across the face.

"That's for being rude to my mother," he said. "And what were you doing behind that curtain?"

"Just reading."

"Show me the book."

I handed him the book of birds.

"You have no right to read our books," he taunted. "You're no better than a beggar, mother says. You have no money, and she only looks after you out of the goodness of her heart. Now, I'll teach you to go rummaging through my things. Go and stand over there, facing the door."

I did as he said, then waited, flinching. Sure enough, he hurled the heavy book at me. It hit my head and I fell, cutting my face on the doorframe.

Suddenly my fear had gone, and I was filled with burning anger. I picked myself up, and through my tears I screamed at him, "You're a wicked monster! You're no better than a murderer – or a slave-driver!"

He ran headlong at me and grabbed my hair; I flailed and scratched at his face with my hands as he wrestled me to the ground. "You little rat!" he shouted again. "Help! Help! Jane is attacking me!"

The next thing I knew, the servants had pulled us

apart, and Mrs. Reed was standing over me.

"Dear, dear," said Abbott, shaking her head. "What a fury, to fly at master John like that!"

"Such a little firebrand!" Bessie tutted.

"Take her away," said Mrs. Reed, "and lock her in the Red Room. That will teach her a lesson."

The Red Room was the biggest, grandest bedroom in Gateshead Hall. It had a red carpet, red damask drapery, and a dark mahogany four-poster bed with red velvet curtains. But nobody slept there. Nobody wanted to. It was here, nine years before, in that very bed, that Mr. Reed had died. Ever since then, the room had been unused, and I had often heard the servants whispering that it was haunted.

Bessie and Abbott had to use all their strength to drag me up the stairs and force me through the door. I only stopped struggling when they threatened to tie me to a chair if I didn't behave.

"I never saw such a disagreeable child," said Abbott, straightening her pinafore.

"Miss Eyre, you should be grateful to Mrs. Reed for keeping you," said Bessie, in a kinder voice. "If you don't behave, she might send you away, and then where would you be?"

"Come on, Bessie," said Abbott. "You'd better say your prayers, Miss, and ask for forgiveness." They left, and I heard the click of the door being locked.

Left alone, holding furiously onto the chair I had been pushed into, I turned the afternoon's events over and over in my mind. Why was I treated so unfairly? Why was John Reed allowed to be rude and violent to me, while I was punished for simply defending myself? And why did everyone adore selfish, spoiled Georgiana and Eliza, and hate me, even though I tried to be good? Was it because they were pretty, with their golden curls and silk dresses, while I was poor and plain?

It was starting to get dark in the Red Room, and I had no candle. It was cold too, as the fire was never lit. As the daylight faded, the furniture began to form frightening shadows all around me. I thought about Mr. Reed, lying in his grave. He had been my uncle – my mother's brother. When my parents had died, I was a baby, and my uncle Reed had brought me to live at Gateshead Hall. Bessie had told me that Mrs. Reed only continued to look after me because, just before his death, Mr. Reed had made her promise that she would.

He would have been kind to me, I was sure. Perhaps his spirit was watching, and was angry about the way they bullied me. Perhaps – I gripped the chair more tightly, and felt a chill of terror – perhaps his ghost really did live in this room.

The thought of seeing a ghost, even kind Mr. Reed's ghost, filled me with dread. I shrank back against the wall and stared into the darkness in a petrified panic, convinced a phantom figure was about to loom into view.

At that moment, a strange, swaying spot of light glanced in through the window, and began to hover slowly across the ceiling towards me.

17

Looking back, I know it was probably nothing more than a footman carrying a lantern across the lawn. But, in my terrified state of mind, I believed it was the ghost. I heard a bloodcurdling scream, and realized that it was me who was screaming. I flung myself out of my seat, rushed over to the door and desperately shook the handle.

I heard footsteps running along the hallway, the door was unlocked, and Bessie opened it. I clung to her as if she was my own mother. "Let me out, Bessie, please, please let me go to my own bed!" I sobbed.

"What is it?" she said, holding me tight. "What a dreadful scream!"

"There was a light, and I thought a ghost would come..."

"A likely story." It was Mrs. Reed, striding down the hall in her nightgown and cap. "Bessie, I told you to leave Jane alone."

"But she screamed so loud, ma'am..."

"She's trying to trick us," Mrs. Reed said. "I can't abide deceitful little girls." And she tore me away from Bessie, pushed me back into the darkness and slammed the door.

Left alone once more, I curled up on the floor and sobbed until I could hardly breathe. In the end I must have fallen unconscious, as that was the last thing I remembered.

Escape

When I awoke, I was aware of being somewhere warm and soft. There seemed to be a red glow nearby, with thick black bars across it, and I could hear muffled voices around me. I felt hands helping me to sit up, and when I opened my eyes properly, I saw that I was in my own bed. The glow came from the fireplace, and there were candles burning. It was night. Bessie was standing beside me, looking anxious. And sitting in a chair by the bed was a sprightly, bright-eyed old man. I recognized him as Mr. Lloyd, the apothecary.

"Do you know who I am, Jane?" he asked.

"You are Mr. Lloyd. You come when the servants are ill," I said. If Mrs. Reed herself or her own children ever fell sick, she called a proper doctor.

"Well, I think she'll be alright after all," Mr. Lloyd smiled, holding my hand. "I'll come back tomorrow. In the meantime, make sure she stays warm."

After seeing him out, Bessie returned. "Is there anything I can do for you, Miss Eyre?" she asked softly. "Would you like a bite to eat – or some milk?"

"No thank you," I said, puzzled. Why was she being so nice to me?

"Then I'll go to bed myself – it's after midnight," she said. "But you can call me if you need me."

"Bessie, what happened?" I asked. "Am I ill?"

"You fell into a faint with crying, in the Red Room," said Bessie. "You'll be better soon."

The next day, I sat wrapped in a blanket by the fire, feeling miserable. The Reeds were out visiting friends in their carriage, and I should have been happy. Instead, I felt as if my spirit had been broken.

Bessie came in with a pastry tart for me. She had put it on a beautiful little plate, decorated with flowers and birds. I had always loved this plate, but I had never been allowed to touch it. Now, I could find no pleasure in it, and I had no appetite.

Then Bessie asked if I wanted to read a book. I chose *Gulliver's Travels* – but, when I opened it, the same feeling came over me. The stories and pictures I had loved meant nothing, and I put the book aside.

At midday, Mr. Lloyd returned, as he had promised, and asked Bessie how I was.

"She's doing very well, sir," she replied.

"Then what's wrong, Jane? You've been crying."

"I daresay she's upset because she couldn't go out in the carriage with the others," said Bessie.

I was outraged at this suggestion. "No!" I said indignantly. "I was only crying because I was sad."

"Sad? But why?"

"I suppose she's still sore from her fall," said Bessie.

"I did *not* fall," I said. "I was knocked down. But that's not why I'm sad."

"Why, then?" asked the apothecary.

Just then, the bell rang, calling the servants to their lunch. I could tell Bessie wanted to stay and listen, but the rules were strict and she must not be late.

"Now then," said Mr. Lloyd, when she had gone. "What do you have to be sad about?"

I wanted to tell him everything, but I knew that telling tales was wrong. Finally I said, "I was locked in a room where there was a ghost."

"Dear me!" laughed Mr. Lloyd. "You don't believe in ghosts, do you – a sensible girl like you?"

"And I have no mother or father..." I went on.

"But you have a kind aunt who cares for you, and cousins to play with. And aren't you grateful to have a beautiful house like Gateshead Hall to live in?"

"This is not my house," I said, "and they say I have less right to be here than a servant. I hate it here."

"What nonsense," said Mr. Lloyd. "I can't believe you would want to leave such a splendid place."

"I would," I said, deadly serious. "If I had anywhere else to go, I would leave this second."

Now I could see that Mr. Lloyd believed me. His eyes narrowed, and he looked thoughtful.

"Hmm," he said. "Would you like to go to school?"

School! I had never been to school in my life, and hardly knew what it meant. John Reed went to school, for weeks at a time, and said he hated it.

But Bessie had told me that she had once worked for a family where the girls went to school, and they could paint and sew, and sing and play the piano, and read books in French. Books! If I went to school, I would be allowed to read all kinds of books. And it would mean leaving Gateshead Hall behind at last.

"Yes," I said. "Yes, I would like to go to school."

"Well then," he said. "I will speak to Mrs. Reed, and we'll see what we can do."

After that day, I was kept even more separate from the others. I had to eat my meals alone, and Mrs. Reed told John, Eliza and Georgiana not to speak to me. I spent more time with the servants than I did with the Reeds. Eventually, Bessie started to give me dusting and tidying jobs to do, to keep me busy.

I waited to hear if I was going to school, but nothing happened. I waited through November and December; Christmas came and went. I was excluded from the parties and celebrations. I would wait in my room, listening to the sound of the piano, the clink of glasses and the hum of conversation below. Sometimes, Bessie would smuggle a cake or pastry from the feast, and bring it to me upstairs.

Then, one day in January, I was in the nursery, tidying up toys, when Bessie came in. "Miss Jane!" she said. "Haven't you finished that yet? Leave it be, now, and take off your pinafore. Have you brushed your hair this morning?" She bustled me over to the washstand, scrubbed my face and quickly brushed my hair. "Mrs. Reed wants to see you in the drawing room," she said. "Hurry now."

I knocked on the drawing room door, and went in. Mrs. Reed was sitting in her usual chair, and standing opposite her was a huge, grim-faced man with bushy eyebrows, wearing a black suit.

"This is the little girl I wrote to you about," Mrs. Reed told him.

"Come here," he said. "What is your name, child?"

"Jane Eyre, sir."

"And are you a good girl, Jane Eyre?"

I wasn't sure what to say. I thought I was good, but I knew no one else in the house agreed.

"The less said about that, the better," snorted Mrs. Reed. "In short, she's deceitful, dishonest and wicked."

"I'm sorry to hear it," said the man coldly. "Do you know where wicked people go, Jane, after they die?"

"They go to Hell?" I offered.

"Indeed they do," he said. "Is that what you want to happen to you?"

"No, sir," I said.

"So what must you do to avoid it?"

I was at a loss. I knew I couldn't try any harder to be good, so I said: "I must take care not to die, sir."

This was not the right answer. The man sighed.

"Do you read your Bible, Miss Eyre?"

I could answer this. "Yes!" I said happily. "I love Revelations, and the Book of Daniel, and Genesis."

"What about the Psalms?"

"I don't like them," I said, truthfully.

"Oh, wicked child! I know a little boy, younger than you, who knows six Psalms by heart. When asked what he would prefer, a ginger cake or a Psalm to learn, he says, 'Oh, the Psalm, please. Angels sing Psalms. I wish to be like a little angel.' He then gets two cakes as a reward for his goodness."

I thought this boy sounded a lot more deceitful than me, but I said nothing.

Mrs. Reed broke the silence. "Mr. Brocklehurst," she said. "I don't know if you'll be able to do anything with her, but you're welcome to try. You'll need to keep a close eye on her, as she's a cunning little thing." I burned with indignation and anger. She went on: "Jane needs to learn her humble place in this world. She is far too proud for her own good."

"You need have no fears on that account, Madam," replied Mr. Brocklehurst. "I have no

patience for the sin of pride. I take great care to instil humility in all the girls at Lowood, and they have no ideas above their station. Why, just the other day, my daughter Augusta visited the school. Immediately afterwards she remarked: 'Papa, how dull and plain the Lowood girls are, with their hair combed behind their ears and their homely pinafores. They stared at me as if they had never seen a silk gown before!' "

"It sounds perfect for Miss Eyre," Mrs. Reed declared. "If it suits you, Mr. Brocklehurst, I will send her as soon as possible. She will stay full-time, and spend the vacations there too."

When she returned from seeing Mr. Brocklehurst out, I stared at her with barely concealed fury.

"Go back upstairs, Jane," she ordered. But I was not ready to go upstairs. She had lied about me, and ruined my chances of making a new start at school. Now I knew I was going, I couldn't resist giving her a piece of my mind.

"I am *not* deceitful," I said. "I am *not* dishonest. If I were, I would lie and say I liked you, and I do not. I hate you. And I hate your son, and your stupid girls as well. They are the liars, not me."

She stared at me with her icy eyes. "Have you anything more to add?" she asked coldly, as if she were speaking to an adult, not a child. Her sarcastic tone made me even more furious. I trembled from head to toe with rage as I shouted: "Yes I do! I am glad you are not my true relation. I will never call you aunt again as long as I live. I will never come and visit you. And if anyone ever asks me about you,

I will tell them how cruel you were to me, and that the very thought of you makes me sick."

"How *dare* you say that?" she gasped.

"I dare say it," I retorted, "because it is the *truth*. I will always remember how you pushed me back into the Red Room, even though I cried and begged for mercy. And why were you punishing me? Because *your* son had knocked me down. You pretend to be respectable, but in private you're cruel and unfair. So *you* are the deceitful one, not me. What would Mr. Reed say if he could see the way you've treated me?"

I expected her to scream at me. But she didn't. When I mentioned her dead husband, I saw guilt and fear flash behind her eyes, and she turned away.

"Go upstairs, Jane," she said quietly. "Bessie will help you pack your things."

Bessie came into my room before dawn to wake me, but I was already dressed and ready to go. She tried to make me have some bread and milk, but I couldn't eat a thing.

As I walked along the hallway and down the stairs of Gateshead Hall, I passed Mrs. Reed's room. I had no wish to go in and say goodbye to her. Bessie and I stepped out of the front door and into the darkness – I with my small case, Bessie with a lantern. It was dark and cold outside, and the lanternlight reflected off the wet gravel as we crunched down the driveway to the road.

At the lodge house, the porter's wife was up and lighting her fire for the day. She came out to chat to

Bessie; I could already hear the sound of the public coach thundering towards us in the distance.

"Is she going by herself?" the porter's wife asked.

"Yes, fifty miles, all on her own," said Bessie.

The coach lights came into view, and the horses pulled to a halt. My suitcase was taken from me and hoisted onto the roof. I hugged Bessie tightly, and she kissed me on the cheek. Then the guard picked me up out of her arms, and lifted me inside. The door slammed shut between us.

"Be sure to take good care of her!" called Bessie, as the horses were urged on, the wheels began to move and, alone and uncertain, I was carried away to my new life.

Lowood

The journey took all day, and I remember very little about it, except that it felt like the longest day I had ever lived through. We passed through town after town. In one of them, the coach stopped at an inn for the passengers to have dinner. The guard wanted me to eat too, but I had no appetite.

As the damp, misty afternoon wore on and faded into dusk, I began to feel I was entering a different world. There were no more towns. Instead we were surrounded by huge hills, looming high over the road. The coach descended into a dark, wooded valley, and night enveloped us. Soon I could see nothing but inky blackness beyond the rain-streaked windows; but I could still hear the wind rushing through the trees all around us.

At last I fell asleep, waking only when the coach came to a stop. The door was opened, and I saw a servant standing in the rain.

"Is there a little girl named Jane Eyre here?" she asked. The guard lifted me out, my suitcase was handed down, and seconds later the coach was gone.

As my eyes adjusted to the darkness, I saw a high stone wall in front of us. The servant opened a door, and I followed her through it. She led me up a wet, pebbly path, through a doorway, along a passage, and into a silent room, where a bright fire burned in the grate. There she left me alone.

There was no candle, but I could see the room dimly by the firelight. It had patterned wallpaper, thick carpets, and paintings on the wall. I was peering at one of them when the door opened, and two people came in. The first was a tall lady, with dark hair, carrying a lamp. She had an elegant, serious air, and I thought she looked kind.

"This child is very young to be sent alone," she said at once, coming up to me and placing a hand on my shoulder. She turned to her companion. "She had better go to bed soon, Miss Miller; she looks very tired. Are you tired, Jane?"

"A little, ma'am."

"And hungry too, I'm sure. Let her have some supper before she goes to bed. Is this the first time you have been away from home?"

I explained to her that I did not really have a home, and was an orphan. She asked more questions: how old I was, and if I could read and write. Then she said she hoped I would be good, and went away.

I followed Miss Miller through corridors and hallways, until I became aware of the the low hum of human voices. It grew louder and louder, until at last we came through a heavy double door into a wide, high-ceilinged room. There were two long tables on each side, and around them, on wooden benches, sat girls of every age — from nine or ten, no

older than myself, up to 17 or 18 years old. There were in fact only about 80 girls at the school, but to me, on that first night, they seemed countless. They were all dressed alike, in brown wool dresses and plain white pinafores. They were studying; the humming I had heard was the sound of them murmuring to themselves, repeating over and over the things they had to learn by heart.

Miss Miller sat me at a table, then marched up to the top of the room, where she gave a loud order:

"Monitors! Fetch the supper-trays!"

Immediately four older girls, one from each table, got up and left the room. When they returned, each carried a water jug and a cup on a wooden tray. At each table, the cup was filled with water and passed around. My turn came, and I took a much-needed drink. Each table also had a large oatcake, which was broken up and passed around. But I still couldn't eat.

When supper was over, Miss Miller read prayers, and then we all filed upstairs, two by two, to a dormitory. By now I was so exhausted, I hardly noticed what the room was like. I was shown to my bed, put on my nightgown and fell asleep in seconds.

The next time I opened my eyes, a loud bell was ringing and girls were up and dressing all around me. It was still dark, and freezing cold in the dormitory. I dressed quickly and waited for my turn at the washstand. But I had hardly begun to wash my face when the bell rang again, I was called into line, and we marched back downstairs to the schoolroom.

There were four classes, and Miss Miller put me in the youngest. Soon three more teachers arrived, but none of them was the kind, dark-haired lady I had seen the night before.

We said prayers and read from the Bible for an hour, until the day dawned at last. It was time for breakfast, and I was ravenous. I had not eaten a thing since my last evening at Gateshead, two days ago.

At the sound of the breakfast bell, we formed into pairs again to go into the refectory. This was a bare hall near the schoolroom, furnished with two long tables. A bowl of something steaming hot was set in every place. But a bitter, rotten smell filled the air, and I could hear the tall girls at the front whispering that the porridge was burned again.

"Silence," snapped one of the teachers, a short woman with a sour, scowling face. We took our places, and began to eat. I was so hungry that I swallowed several mouthfuls before the revolting, gluey taste of the burned porridge made me stop. All around me, the other girls struggled to eat it, but despite their hunger, they could not.

I was at the back of the group as we filed out again, and I saw one of the teachers try our porridge. She whispered to the others. "It's disgusting!" I heard her say. "How shameful!"

The bell rang for lessons, and we joined our classes again. Miss Miller ordered the monitors to fetch the globes for a geography lesson. But, before we could start, everyone suddenly stood up. The dark-haired lady had reappeared at last.

She walked up and down the benches, inspecting us. I stared at her as she passed by our table. She was tall and graceful, and so beautiful. Her eyes were brown, with long, fine lashes. Her dark chestnut hair was curled and fastened at the sides of her head, and she wore a purple dress with black velvet trimming, and a gleaming golden watch chain at her waist.

Finally, she came to the middle of the room, and stood before us to make an announcement.

"You had a breakfast this morning which was unfit to eat," she said. "It is not good for you to go hungry. I have ordered some bread and cheese to be served after the first lesson."

The other teachers looked surprised and alarmed, but she waved her hand. "I will take full responsibility," she said. And so, after the lesson was over, the delicious fresh bread and cheese was brought in, and we feasted and ate our fill.

Then I was given a cloak and bonnet to wear, and we were sent outside.

Outdoors there was a big, square lawn, with a verandah running alongside it, and cultivation beds, where in the summer we would grow flowers and vegetables. But now, at the end of January, it was cold and dreary. We were allowed to play games, but only a few girls did. The rest huddled in groups to stay warm, and I heard many of them coughing.

I did not know anyone, and I was shy. Everyone ignored me. If I had come from a happy home, a warm and loving family, I might have missed it most now; but I was used to being alone. I stood by myself next to the verandah, clutching my cloak around me, and watched the others playing. Then I looked up at the stone school building. I saw that it had an inscription above the door:

LOWOOD INSTITUTION
THIS HOUSE WAS BUILT IN 1813 BY NAOMI
BROCKLEHURST, OF BROCKLEHURST HALL.

I heard a cough, and turned around. A girl a few years older than me was sitting on a stone bench, reading a book. I leaned over to see what it was called – *Rasselas*. It sounded exotic and exciting, as if it might be about genies and dragons. I wished I had a book to read myself, and I wondered if the girl might lend it to me one day.

As she turned the page, she looked up and saw me watching her. I immediately took my chance to speak. "Is your book interesting?" I asked.

"I like it," she said.

"What's it about?"

She handed me the book to look at, and I turned to the first page, but it wasn't about dragons and genies after all. There were no pictures, and it looked dull. I gave it back, and she was about to return to her reading when I interrupted her again:

"Do you know what that inscription means? What is Lowood Institution?"

"This is," she said. "Your new home."

"Why is it called an institution? Is it different from other schools?"

"It's a charity school," she said, "for orphans. Everyone here has lost one of their parents, or both."

"Who was Naomi Brocklehurst?"

"The lady who founded Lowood, of course. She's dead now, and her son owns the school."

"So that tall lady – the one who ordered the bread and cheese – she's not the owner?"

"Miss Temple? I wish she were! No, she's just the manager – she has to answer to Mr. Brocklehurst."

Mr. Brocklehurst – that cold, cruel man who'd visited Mrs. Reed at Gateshead Hall. "Does he live here?" I asked.

"Oh no, he lives in a big house two miles away, with his family. He's the village clergyman – you'll see him on Sunday, when we go to church."

I asked her about the teachers. The short, sour-faced one was Miss Scatcherd, Miss Smith taught sewing, and an older lady I had seen in the refectory was Madame Pierrot, the French teacher. Miss Miller was Miss Temple's deputy, and Miss Temple was loved by everyone – she was clever, good and kind.

"Are you an orphan too?" I asked finally.

"My mother is dead."

"Are you happy here?"

"You ask too many questions," said the girl, and went back to her book. Soon after that, the bell rang to call us back inside. We had more lessons, and a lunch of watery potato stew with scraps of meat.

During the afternoon, I saw my new friend, who was in an older group, being severely scolded by Miss Scatcherd. I could not see what she had done wrong, but she was sent to stand in the middle of the schoolroom, where everyone could stare at her.

If this had happened to me, I knew I would have fumed with rage and indignation. I would have burned bright red with embarrasment. So I was amazed to see her standing there meekly and quietly, looking at the floor without a hint of rebellion. I did not understand her.

The school day ended with a meal of bread and milk, then half an hour in which the girls could relax and talk as they pleased. Then came studying and preparing for tomorrow's tasks, the water and oatcake supper, prayers, and bed.

My first day at school was over.

Helen Burns

The next day began just like the one before it – except that we could not wash, as the water was frozen solid. The weather had turned even colder, and a freezing wind blew right into the dormitory through the crevices in the ill-fitting windows.

We shivered through our early morning prayers until the breakfast bell. Today, the porridge was not burned, but there still wasn't enough of it. I wished I could have it over again.

Until now I had only watched the lessons; today I had to take part in them. I was asked questions, and had to learn things by heart. I wasn't used to it, and I struggled to keep up. I was relieved when, in the afternoon, we were sent to Miss Smith for sewing. She gave me a long piece of muslin, and told me to sew a hem along one side, which I could do easily.

Most of the other girls were sewing too, but Miss Scatcherd's class was still studying. It was an English history lesson. The rest of us were sitting so quietly that we could hear every word – Miss Scatcherd's questions, and each girl's response. I could see the girl I had talked to on the verandah: in fact, Miss Scatcherd seemed to be scolding her constantly.

"Burns," she would snap (the teachers called us all by our last names). "You are sitting awkwardly – sit up straight!" Or: "Burns, don't scowl like that!"

When it came to being tested on what they had learned, Burns seemed to do far better than the rest. She knew all the facts about the reign of King Charles that no one else could remember, but still Miss Scatcherd didn't praise her. "Burns, you haven't cleaned your nails this morning!" she nagged.

"Why doesn't she tell her," I wondered to myself, "that the water was frozen and *nobody* could clean their nails?" But Burns stayed meek and silent.

Just then, Miss Smith came to help me with my sewing. She asked me questions – how much could I sew? Could I knit, or darn, or do blanket stitch? Had I been to school before? She was kind, but her chattering meant I had to stop concentrating on the class, and couldn't see for a while what was going on.

When I looked back at last, it seemed Burns had been sent to fetch something. She went over to the cupboard where the books were stored, and returned with a bundle of long twigs, which she handed to Miss Scatcherd. I watched in horror as she unlaced her pinafore at the shoulder and pulled it aside, and the teacher unhesitatingly gave her twelve sharp lashes on the side of her neck.

I shook with anger and indignation, and could almost feel the pain myself. With each stroke, I flinched, and tears came to my eyes. But Burns did not flinch. Throughout her punishment, she kept her usual calm, humble expression. Even for this, she was scolded. "Hard, unfeeling girl!" Miss Scatcherd said. "You are beyond correcting; take the rod away!"

I watched Burns as she returned to the cupboard. When she came back, she had her handkerchief in hand, and I could see that she had cried a little.

That evening, after our bread and milk, I wandered around the tables. I had decided that this was the best part of the day: the fires were stoked up, and we were free to relax and talk for a whole hour. I was hoping to be able to talk to the girl again.

At last I found her sitting by a hearth, still reading the same book. She was just finishing it. I sat down beside her on the floor and, when she had closed the book, I asked: "What is your name, besides Burns?"

"Helen."

"Where did you come here from?"

"From a long way north, almost as far as Scotland."

"You must wish you could go back."

"No," she said, frowning at me. "Why should I? I was sent here for my own good, to be educated."

"But Miss Scatcherd is so cruel to you."

"She's not cruel," said Helen, "she's just strict. I have many faults, and she wants to correct them."

"But she beat you!" I cried. "And you had done nothing wrong! If it had been me, I'd have snatched the rod from her hand and broken it in two!"

"You probably wouldn't," said Helen wisely, "and anyway, if you had, you would have been expelled, and that would have upset your family. It's better to endure pain yourself, than to cause problems for other people. Besides, the Bible teaches us to love our enemies, and return good for evil."

"But she humiliated you! I couldn't bear it!"

"You are here: it's your duty to bear it," she said.

I stared at her open-mouthed. How could she be so forgiving? "Well, Miss Scatcherd is wrong," I said, finally. "You don't seem to have any faults at all."

"Of course I do!" she laughed. "I'm untidy, and careless, I forget the rules, I read new books when I should be learning my lessons."

"But Miss Temple is not cruel to you like Miss Scatcherd, is she?" I asked cunningly. "So perhaps you don't deserve it after all."

At the mention of Miss Temple's name, Helen smiled. "Miss Temple is full of goodness," she said, "and is always gentle and kind. But, even then, I can't manage to behave properly. Which just goes to show that I do have faults. I am full of them."

Just then, one of the oldest girls came up to us.

"Helen Burns, you are to put away your books, and put your clothes drawer in order, this minute, Miss Scatcherd says." Helen got up without a reply, and immediately went to do as she was told.

I was left by the fire, puzzling to myself. It seemed that I had made a friend, though I didn't understand her very well, and she certainly didn't agree with my views on life. But I liked her. And at Lowood I was going to need whatever friends I could find.

The next three months continued much the same, and I tried hard to get used to the daily tasks, the routine, and the endless rules. The freezing weather stayed through February and March, and I had painful chilblains on my feet. And I never had enough food. As the portions were so small, some of the bigger girls would bully the little ones for their bread. I was often forced to share what I had between two or three others, managing to keep only a tiny morsel for myself, which I would eat in tears.

Sundays were the worst days of all. Although we had no proper outdoor boots, we had to walk two miles in the snow to Brocklebridge Church, in the nearby village of Lowton, where Mr. Brocklehurst was the preacher. We were chilled to the bone on the way, and then had to spend the day in the freezing stone church, getting colder still. Instead of going back for lunch, we were given a tiny scrap of bread and cold meat before the sermons resumed. When we came home in the evening, faces blasted by the icy wind, we longed for the heat of the fire — but the bigger girls always pushed their way to the front, and we little ones were left to crouch behind them, pulling our pinafores around our skinny arms.

In my first weeks at Lowood, Mr. Brocklehurst was away on business. But one fateful afternoon in February, I looked up from my lesson to see a tall, black-clad figure passing the window. Sure enough, two minutes later, as if by a secret signal, everyone stood to attention, and Mr. Brocklehurst strode into the schoolroom. I had dreaded seeing him, because I remembered Mrs. Reed lying to him about me, and I was afraid he would make an example of me.

At first, it seemed I didn't need to worry. He began by taking Miss Temple aside, and complaining to her about the state of the stockings on the washing line. "They are full of holes, ma'am!" I heard him say. "See that they are properly darned. I have ordered more darning needles. And furthermore, Miss Temple, on looking over my accounts, I find that a quantity of bread and cheese was sent for, not three weeks since. What is this? Who ordered this luxury?"

"I did, sir," said Miss Temple. She explained to him that the porridge had been burned, and that the breakfast was inedible.

Mr. Brocklehurst was not impressed. "You are aware, madam," he said, his voice growing louder, "that I do not intend to accustom these girls to habits of luxury and indulgence, but to teach them humility and hardiness. They should be able to withstand the occasional spoiling of a meal. Indeed, instead of rewarding them with a delicate treat, you should have taken the opportunity to lecture them upon the suffering of our Lord, and fed their immortal souls instead of their bodies."

Miss Temple did not reply, but stared straight ahead with a fixed expression. Mr. Brocklehurst turned away from her and looked around the room. His eyes fell on a girl in the second class, and he blinked as if blinded by lightning. "Miss Temple!" he snapped. "What is – why does that girl have her hair curled – curled all over?"

"It is Julia Severn, sir," said Miss Temple. "Her hair curls naturally."

"Naturally, madam? We are not here to conform to nature, and run wild like animals. Girls must be taught to wear their hair modestly, and dress plainly. That hair must be cut off. All these braids and curls will be cut short. I will send a barber soon."

"Yes, sir," said Miss Temple, and held her handkerchief in front of her mouth. I was sure she was hiding a smile at his ridiculous pomposity.

Just then, the door opened again, and in walked three ladies – two young, and one older.

I wished they had arrived a little earlier to hear Mr. Brocklehurst's lecture on dressing modestly. All three were wearing gorgeous velvet and silk dresses, and fur-trimmed cloaks. The two girls had ostrich-feather hats, and beneath them tumbled masses of blonde, elaborately curled hair.

Miss Temple politely went to welcome them, addressing the older woman as Mrs. Brocklehurst. I now realized they must be Mr. Brocklehurst's wife and daughters. They began talking to Miss Temple as well, making complaints and finding fault with the housekeeping.

Meanwhile, I was trying to make sure I wouldn't be noticed. Trying to appear as if I was studying my numbers, I leaned back on the bench, and held my slate so that it blocked Mr. Brocklehurst's view of my face. My plan would have worked, except that my slate, being held at an awkward angle, slipped from my hand and smashed on the floor.

"A careless child!" Mr. Brocklehurst cried, whirling around. When he saw me, my worst fears came true.

"Aha!" he announced. "I have a word or two to say regarding this particular child. Come here."

I was frozen with fear, but the other girls pushed me up and I stumbled into the middle of the room. Mr. Brocklehurst told a monitor to lift me onto a stool, so that I stood almost face to face with him.

"You see this girl?" he began, addressing the whole room. "She may look like an ordinary little girl. She may look harmless. But I regret to tell you that she is already a servant of the devil. She is an evil, mischievous little liar, with a violent temper. This I learned from her kind benefactress, who was forced to send her away to school to protect her own, pure children from the corrupting influence of this ungrateful wretch." He paused and paced around the room, while his daughters stared at me in horror.

"I must warn you all," Mr. Brocklehurst continued, "not to associate with her. Shun her company; exclude her from your games; do not speak to her or look upon her. Teachers, you must be on your guard against her tricks, and punish her severely when she misbehaves. It is the only way to save her soul — if indeed it can be saved."

Then he returned to his family and they took their leave. Before closing the door behind him, he called: "She is to stay there for a further half-hour."

I was so mortified, furious and ashamed that I didn't know how I could bear to stand there for another second, let alone a half-hour. My face burned and my eyes brimmed with tears, and my outraged feelings of injustice rose up in my throat, so that I felt I could hardly breathe. I stared helplessly at the wall on the other side of the room, as I couldn't bear the thought of anyone looking me in the eye.

But then I realized someone was coming near me, walking right past my stool. I looked down. It was Helen. She had made some excuse to fetch a book or a pencil, and as she passed by, she looked up at me with a quick, friendly smile. She ran her errand, then came back the same way, and smiled at me again. This one small gesture gave me the strength I needed. I controlled my fury, lifted my head up high and resolved to endure my punishment with dignity.

The Sickness

It was less than half an hour until five o'clock and the end of lessons. So I was still standing there, on my stool in the middle of the room, when the bell rang for tea, and everyone put away their books and crowded into the refectory. I was left alone and miserable, knowing I would miss my longed-for bread and milk.

I watched the clock on the wall, and when the half-hour had completely passed, I climbed down stiffly. Then I crumpled onto the schoolroom floor, and began to cry.

I had tried so hard. I had meant to be so good, and to do so well. And I *had* been doing well – that very morning, I had reached the top of my class. Miss Miller and Miss Smith had praised me for my hard work. The other girls had accepted me, and now treated me as an equal. And Miss Temple had said that, if I continued to improve for another two months, she would let me start learning French and drawing, like the big girls. And now Mr. Brocklehurst had ruined everything.

No one would speak to me now – no one would want to know me – and the teachers would think I had deceived them all this time. I would never be allowed to learn French and drawing. I lowered my head onto the floorboards and cried until my tears soaked into them.

Then I heard someone approaching, and I sat up. By the dim light of the fading fire, I saw that it was Helen Burns. She was carrying my bread and milk.

"Come on, eat something," she said kindly, and sat down next to me, setting my cup and plate on the floor. But I was too ashamed to eat in front of her.

"Helen," I sobbed, "how can you come near me now? Everyone thinks I'm a liar."

"No," she said, "not everyone. Eighty people heard him call you that, but there are millions of people in the world."

"But the people here are the only ones I know. And now they all hate me."

"You're wrong, Jane, they don't hate you. They're probably sorry for you."

"How can they be, after what he said?"

"Jane, Mr. Brocklehurst is not a god. In fact, no one here likes him. If he had held you up as a shining example of goodness – well, then perhaps you would be hated. As it is, you might find people avoid you for a day or two, for the sake of appearances, but they admire you in their hearts. And besides..."

"What?" I said. She took my hand in hers, and looked me in the eye. "What would it matter if all the world hated you, if you knew in your heart you were innocent? Only God can judge us, Jane – no matter what other people think. Life in this world is short — but when you die, you will be judged on your true inner goodness, and will go to Heaven." As she said this, her eyes seemed to glow with a fervent light.

I supposed she was right, but I couldn't deny it — it *did* matter to me what other people thought. I wanted to have friends and laughter and fun — wanted to belong to the group. Helen was a truly good person, but I sensed a loneliness in her.

As I stared at her in the half-light, she suddenly turned aside and began to cough. She coughed hard for several minutes, and for a while I forgot my sorrows and went to put my arms around her.

As I hugged her shaking shoulders, someone else came into the deserted schoolroom. It was Miss Temple.

"Jane Eyre?" she said. "I came here to find you — I would like you to visit me in my rooms. And Helen, since you are here, you may come too."

We got up and followed her away from the schoolroom, through parts of the building I never normally saw, along a passage and up a staircase, until we reached her private apartment. There was a good fire burning, and cosy armchairs around it.

When we had sat down, Miss Temple asked: "Do you feel better now, Jane? Have you cried away all your sadness?"

"No," I said. "I can never do that. I have been wrongly accused, and now everyone will think I'm evil. While they think that, I can never be happy."

"Well," Miss Temple said, "I shall only judge you

on the way you behave here. If you continue to be good and work hard, I will be satisfied."

I stared at her, unable to believe her kindness.

"And now," she said, "I would like you to tell me about this benefactress of yours. When someone is accused of a crime in court, Jane, he is always allowed to defend himself. I would like to hear your side of the story."

And so I told her all about Mrs. Reed, and John Reed, and the Red Room, and all the things that happened at Gateshead Hall. But, as I did so, I tried to take a leaf out of Helen's book, and to be calm instead of angry and resentful. I told the story as fairly as I could, and included all my own faults.

During my tale, I mentioned Mr. Lloyd, the apothecary who had suggested I go to school. When I had finished, Miss Temple said: "Thank you, Jane.

I know Mr. Lloyd, and I will write to him. If his description of events matches yours, I will know you are not a liar, and I will clear your name, and tell the whole school you are innocent. But," she added, "I believe you already. I know you are a good girl."

Then she turned to Helen, and asked how she was. Helen told her that she had coughed a lot that day, but the pain in her chest was a little better.

"Well, you girls are my guests tonight, so you will have tea with me," said Miss Temple finally. She ordered a tray of tea and toast to be brought up.

When the kitchen maid arrived with the tray, we saw that there were plates and teacups for three, but only one slice of toast. Miss Temple sent for more, but the cook would not provide it. She was too afraid of Mr. Brocklehurst finding out.

But as soon as we were left alone, Miss Temple opened a cupboard, and took out a whole fruitcake with nuts on top, wrapped in wax paper.

What an earthly heaven I was in that night! The china teacups looked so pretty in the firelight, with their patterns of tiny flowers. The fragrant steam from the teapot, the aroma of hot toast, and the sight of the thick slices of cake on the plates filled me with joy. As we feasted, and I listened to Helen talking to Miss Temple about French books and faraway places, I couldn't think of a time when I had been happier. Not only was I eating well for the first time in weeks, but I was with beautiful, kind, wise Miss Temple, and I felt safe and warm.

Just a week later, Miss Temple stood before the

school to make an announcement. She had made inquiries, she told us, and she had discovered, from a reliable source, that the allegations made against Miss Jane Eyre were false. Everyone applauded, and all the teachers hugged me. My name was cleared.

From that day onward, I resolved to work harder than ever. Soon I was put up to the next class, and, as I had been promised, started to learn French and drawing. It seemed that nothing could go wrong.

As spring drew on, the conditions at Lowood became easier to bear. It grew warmer, the snow melted, and my poor, red, swollen feet began to heal at last. At first the snowdrops, then the crocuses, daffodils and golden-eyed pansies flowered in the garden, and the trees burst into leaf. And I realized that, in spring, the countryside around the school was beautiful too. There was a clear, babbling stream nearby, and Lowood stood in the middle of a pretty wooded valley, dotted with primroses and surrounded by high hills, purple with heather.

In fact, this beautiful valley was soon to become my playground, a place where I could roam freely from morning till night, and lie in the sun or paddle in the water as I wished. You might wonder how this could be, when our school day was so full of rules and restrictions. But that spring, everything changed.

Lowood may have had a beautiful setting, but it was not a healthy one. The valley, surrounded by its circle of hills, formed a kind of basin where a heavy fog gathered every morning. It floated into the school, breathing dampness and sickness into our lungs. If we had all been strong and well-fed, it wouldn't have mattered so much. But, weakened by a poor diet and a cold winter, more than half of the girls fell victim to typhus. This disease brought on a terrible, wasting fever, and those who suffered from it were confined to their beds, hardly able to eat, move or speak.

The school turned itself into a temporary hospital. The teachers spent every moment looking after the sick; lessons were cancelled, and those of us who remained healthy were sent to play in the sun outside, as far away as possible from the germ-laden sickroom, with no one to watch or scold us.

A few girls, those with families who could look after them, were sent home to avoid the plague. Others were sent home to die. And some died at the school. There were hastily arranged burials; some of the lovely spring flowers in the garden ended up as a humble decoration for the coffins. Gloom and the smell of death hung over the sickroom beds.

But for those of us who were not ill, things were better than before. The invalids did not eat much, so there was more food for the rest. Mr. Brocklehurst was too afraid to visit, in case he caught the disease, and the teachers and servants were free to be kind to us. They gave us slices of pie, apples and parcels of bread and cheese to take out on our explorations. They let us ramble through the woods and across the moors all day, playing and hiding, finding wild flowers and herbs, reading, drawing or talking.

I found a large, flat stone in the middle of the stream, where I would have a picnic every day with my friend Mary Ann. She was a bright, funny girl, who loved to tell stories and laugh out loud. I loved to ask questions and listen to her tales, and so we got on famously.

But why, you might ask, wasn't I with Helen? What had happened to my first and dearest friend?

The answer was that she was gravely ill. She was not in the sickroom. She had been taken to a room upstairs, I didn't know where, and hidden away from the rest of us. She did not have typhus, but an even more serious disease – consumption. Her coughing had been the first sign of her fate. Over the previous months she had grown thin and pale, and now, inside her chest, her lungs were rotting away.

One night, Mary Ann and I came back at dusk, and saw the doctor's pony at the gate. Mary Ann went inside, while I went to my patch of garden to plant some forest herbs I had collected. The ground was still warm, and the garden was filled with the evening scent of grass and petals. After I had done my gardening, I stayed outside for a while, breathing in the soft air and admiring the rising moon.

I was still there when the doctor came out, accompanied by a servant. He climbed onto his pony and took his leave. I ran over to the servant and asked how Helen was. I knew there could be no other reason for the doctor's visit.

"She's very poorly," she replied.

"Was it her the doctor came to see?"

"Yes," she said firmly. I could tell she didn't want to reveal any more.

"What does he say about her?"

She looked at me. "He says she'll not be here long," she said at last.

I knew instantly what this meant. It did not mean that Helen was about to go home to her father. It meant she was close to death. She would soon be going to that place she had spoken of – where she would be judged on her inner goodness alone.

"Where is she?" I asked the servant.

"She's in Miss Temple's room."

"May I go and visit her?"

"Oh, no, child!" she exclaimed. "It's no business for one so young as you. It's time for you to come inside now, before you catch a cold." She bustled me in and closed the door.

I knew I wouldn't be able to sleep until I had seen Helen. I put on my nightgown and climbed into bed like the rest; but I lay awake. I waited for two hours, until everything around me was silent, and I was sure everyone was asleep. Then I got up quietly, put my dress over my nightgown, and crept away to Miss Temple's room.

I pushed the door open gently without knocking, and went in. Miss Temple was not there — she was usually up all night, tending to the sick. The servant I had spoken to earlier was asleep in one of the armchairs, and next to her was a low cot bed, with a human shape lying in it, under heavy blankets.

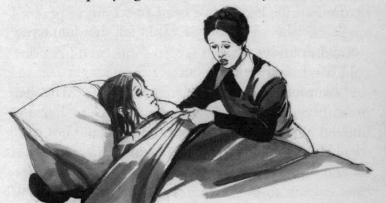

I walked past the sleeping woman and went over to Helen's side. My heart pounded as I leaned over to see her face — what if she was dead already?

Helen was awake. Her face was gaunt and white, but I was relieved to see she looked alert and calm, and recognized me at once.

"Jane?" she whispered, and pulled her hand out from under the bedclothes to hold onto mine.

"Perhaps she won't die," I hoped to myself. "Perhaps they are mistaken."

"Why are you here, Jane?" she asked. "I heard the clock strike eleven."

"I — I heard you were very ill, and I couldn't sleep until I had seen you."

"You've come to say goodbye, then," she smiled, and I tried to force back my brimming tears.

"Please Helen — don't say that."

"Don't worry, Jane. I'm happy. We must all die one day, and I am not in pain. My father is getting married again; he doesn't need me. I am at peace. I am going to God."

I didn't know what to say, so I squeezed her poor, cold hand again.

"Your feet are bare, Jane, you must be cold. Climb in with me." And so I lay down next to her and hugged her, and soon we both fell asleep.

The next thing I knew, it was daytime, and I was woken up by a rocking movement. I was being carried back to the dormitory in the strong arms of one of the nurses.

Later, I learned that Miss Temple had come back to her rooms and found me in the cot with my arms around my friend. Helen was dead.

She was buried in Brocklebridge churchyard, in a pauper's grave with no headstone. But recently, I have been able to have a proper monument carved for her. It is made of grey marble, and bears her name and the word *RESURGAM*, which means: "I will rise again."

Growing Up

Once the typhus had done its worst, it began to disappear – but not before it had made sure Lowood would never be the same again. News of the epidemic spread, the newspapers heard about it, and so did the charitable donors who supported the school. An inquiry was held into how the disease could have taken hold, and soon the public found out about our poor diet, and the cold, crowded, dirty conditions we had been forced to live in. Our rich patrons had been sending enough money to keep us warm, safe and well-fed, but not all of it was being used. In his meanness, Mr. Brocklehurst had been spending only a fraction of the school's funds on the students. Some said he spent the rest on himself and his family; but it could not be proved.

Because of his respectable position, Mr. Brocklehurst was not fired, but his power was removed. A committee of new governors took over the school, and he had to answer to them.

The committee decided to move the school to a new building, in a healthier location on the hillside. We were given better food and bigger helpings, good clothes and proper boots, and more space and time to ourselves. And so Lowood was transformed from a miserable, cruel institution, hardly better than a poorhouse, into a flourishing school with happy, healthy pupils.

I was to stay there for eight years. For the first six, I completed my education, learning history and geography, English, mathematics and music. I became fluent in French, and learned to paint and draw and play the piano, just like the young ladies Bessie had told me about when I was at Gateshead Hall. Then, from the age of 16, I became an assistant teacher to the younger girls.

Throughout those eight years, Miss Temple stayed at Lowood. I owed everything to her. She was a wonderful teacher, helping me with everything I wanted to learn. But she was also like a mother to me, and when I had grown up, she became a dear friend. Over time, I grew to be more like her. I became calmer, more quiet and sensible, and less quick to judge others or fly into a rage.

When I was 18, Miss Temple met her husband-to-be. His name was Mr. Nasmyth, and he was a clergyman. He was kind, thoughtful and intelligent, and she was happy. I thought no man could ever be good enough to deserve a wife like Miss Temple, yet I had to admit that he was almost good enough.

Mr. Nasmyth had a job far off to the west, in another county, and when she married him, Miss Temple had to move away.

How clearly I remember the day she left! The wedding was over; the new Mrs. Nasmyth's bags were packed, and she was wearing an elegant going-away suit of fine dark wool. As the carriage waited, we all stood around and kissed her goodbye, and then she and her new husband climbed inside. I watched, unable to turn my eyes away, as the carriage trundled up the hill and disappeared over its brow; and then Miss Temple was gone.

To mark the occasion, we had been given the day off, so I went up to my room. I walked to and fro, going over the confused feelings inside my head. I was so happy for her, yet I was bereft. I couldn't imagine life without her. And how could the school ever be as good, or the pupils as contented, now she wasn't there to guide and reassure them? I sat down on the bed, and wept a little.

I thought I was only considering how to get over my sorrow, and continue life as normal. But, when I stood up again, and saw that the afternoon was gone, and it was already growing dark, I knew that a much bigger change had taken place.

I felt different. It wasn't just the loss of a friend. Now Miss Temple had gone, the part of me that was like her was fading away too. I felt other feelings stirring in my heart – feelings I remembered from long ago: a desire for adventure, a longing to escape from rules and boundaries, and to explore the world.

I went to the window, opened it, and looked out. I gazed through the gathering dusk, past the outbuildings and grounds, past the garden walls, and over the meadows and treetops to the looming, dark hills in the distance.

I traced the line of the road, where it wound up and around the hills, then disappeared between them. It was the same road that I had come along in the carriage, all those years ago, when I was only ten – and I had never left this valley since. This school, with its rules and customs and routines, a few roads round about, the church and Lowton village – these were my whole life.

I suddenly realized that I longed to be free. I knew that if I were to leave, I would have to work somewhere else. I would probably have to be a servant of some kind. But I had to explore, to travel, to make my own way.

Just then the supper bell rang, and my thoughts were interrupted. I went downstairs, resolving to think more on the matter at bedtime.

Unfortunately, I shared my room with another young teacher, Miss Gryce. She loved to talk endlessly, discussing trivial matters I cared nothing about, and I often struggled to appear interested. That night, when we went up to our room, she insisted on chattering and gossiping away until I thought I would go insane with frustration. I normally found her snoring a nuisance, but tonight I smiled to myself when I heard it begin, for I knew I was free to concentrate on my plans.

I sat up in bed, with a shawl around my shoulders to keep myself warm, and thought hard. What did I want? I wanted a new life. A new job, in a new place – a place where I would meet new people and see new things. I wanted an adventure.

But how? I didn't know anyone who I could ask to give me work. I had only ever been at Gateshead Hall and here, and I knew hardly anything about the world outside. How did people find jobs?

My mind worked faster and faster. Every kind of thought raced around my brain until my head started to throb, but I didn't have an answer. I climbed out of bed and paced around the room quietly; then I pulled back the curtain and looked out at the stars, and started to feel chilly. I got back into bed.

Then it hit me – I could advertize! I knew very little about how to do it, but I could find out. I had often seen notices in the *Herald* newspaper, which the other teachers sometimes bought.

I grew more and more excited as my plan took shape. I would ask for any replies to be addressed to "J.E.", and have them kept at the village post office for me to pick up – that way, no one at the school would know what I was doing. I would write my notice first thing in the morning.

Now I knew what I was going to do, my mind stopped racing, and I settled down to sleep.

By the time the bell rang for lessons the next morning, I had written my notice. It said:

> *A young lady with experience of teaching is looking for a position as governess, to a family with children aged under 14. She is qualified to teach a general range of subjects, including French, Drawing and Music.*

Then I wrote that replies should be sent to J.E., put the address of Lowton post office, and sealed the paper in an envelope.

The letter stayed locked in my drawer all day until teatime, when my duties were over. I told the other teachers I was going to the village to run errands, and set off on the two-mile walk. It was a drizzling, chilly autumn evening, but I brimmed with excitement. I posted my letter, and decided I would go back after a week to see if there were any replies.

How that week dragged on! Every day, I thought about my message going out into the world, and counted the days until I could check my mail.

At last, when the week was up, I made up another errand – having my feet measured for winter boots – and took another evening walk to the village. All the way there, I dreamed about the replies that might be waiting for me, and what they might say.

I pushed open the heavy door of the post office. The old postmistress, in her horn-rimmed spectacles and black mittens, looked at me suspiciously when I asked if there were any letters for J.E. She fumbled through a drawer full of envelopes for what seemed like hours, until I had almost completely lost heart.

Finally, she held up a plain envelope, peered at the address, and, with a distrustful look, handed it over.

"Is there only one?" I asked.

"There are no more," she said firmly.

I left in a hurry; I had to be back by eight, and I only had half an hour to walk the two miles home. I saved the letter to open at my leisure in my room.

When I got back there were things to do. First I had to supervise the study hour, then it was my turn to read prayers, and then the teachers had their supper. Then I had to wait again until Miss Gryce went to sleep, hoping she would drop off before our candle burned down to nothing. By the time I heard her snores, there was just an inch of candle left. I took out my letter and broke the seal.

If Miss J.E. possesses the abilities mentioned, and can give satisfactory references, a situation can be offered her where there is one pupil, a girl of less than ten years old, and where the salary is thirty pounds a year. J.E. is requested to send her full details and references to Mrs. Fairfax, Thornfield Hall, near Millcote.

It was perfect. I read it again and again. From her old-fashioned handwriting, I imagined Mrs. Fairfax to be white-haired, with a black gown and a widow's cap. The little girl was probably her granddaughter, and Thornfield Hall must be her house – how proper and respectable it sounded! I had never been to Millcote, but I knew it was a large manufacturing town. I didn't like the thought of smog and belching chimneys – but then, Thornfield was near Millcote, probably out in the countryside. It was ideal.

The candle sputtered and went out, and I lay down to sleep, holding the letter to my heart.

The next day, I went to the new school manager and told her I had been offered a new position. I asked if she would tell the committee, and find out whether they would give me references.

When Mr. Brocklehurst heard about it, he tried one last trick to thwart me. He insisted that the committee must write to Mrs. Reed, my legal guardian, to ask her permission. A letter came back from her saying that she didn't care what I did.

So, through meetings and discussions that seemed to drag on forever, the committee finally decided that I was free to make my way in the world, and that they would give me good references to reflect my teaching abilities and the honest character I had always shown.

The testimonials were written, and I sent them to Mrs. Fairfax. She wrote back saying she was satisfied with them, and fixing a date, two weeks ahead, for me to start work as a governess at Thornfield Hall.

Thornfield

And so I found myself rattling along a muddy road in the dark, in a slow one-horse buggy, on my way to Thornfield Hall.

It had been a long day. The coach from Lowton to Millcote had taken sixteen hours, after leaving at four o'clock in the morning. Then I had waited for two more hours at an inn in Millcote, before I was collected by Mrs. Fairfax's driver. I had tried to be friendly to him, but he would hardly say a word.

As I bumped around in the tiny buggy, with the driver sitting up on top, I reflected that perhaps Mrs. Fairfax wasn't so grand after all, if this was her carriage. But maybe that was for the best. I was no society lady either, and I was used to things being plain and simple. The last time I had lived among rich people, I reminded myself, I had been miserable. Anyway, I resolved to do my best, come what may. If Mrs. Fairfax turned out to be anything like Mrs. Reed – well, I could go somewhere else.

After what seemed like an age, the buggy drew to a halt at a set of gates. The driver got down and opened them, and we continued up a long drive and stopped in front of the house. Candlelight glowed from one window at the front; the rest were dark. I climbed out of the buggy with my suitcase, and went to the front door, where a maid was waiting.

"Come this way, ma'am," she said politely, and I followed her across the large, square hallway. She opened a door and showed me through.

I couldn't have hoped for a happier scene. The room was small, lit by candles and warmed by a crackling fire. In an armchair sat a plump old lady in a black dress, a cap and a shawl. She was knitting, and at her feet, close to the hearth, curled a contented-looking cat. It was Mrs. Fairfax, just as I had imagined her – except that she looked much friendlier than I had guessed, and not so haughty.

"How do you do, my dear?" she said. "I'm afraid you've had a long journey – John drives so slowly – and you must be freezing. Come to the fireside."

"Mrs. Fairfax?"

"Yes, that's me," she said. She put her knitting aside and got up to help me with my coat and bonnet-strings.

"Please, don't trouble yourself..." I began.

"Oh, it's no trouble – your hands must be numb with cold. Leah," she said to the maid, "will you make Miss Eyre some hot cocoa, and bring us a sandwich or two?"

She was so kind and welcoming, it was as if I were a visiting lady, not the new governess. I couldn't understand it.

"Will I meet Miss Fairfax tonight?" I asked.

"Who? Oh, you mean Miss Varens, your new pupil. That's her name – Adele Varens."

"Is she your relation?"

"No, no – I don't have a family myself," said Mrs. Fairfax, as Leah came in with the tray. I wanted to know exactly how Miss Varens was connected to her, but I was afraid I was asking too many questions.

"Well," Mrs. Fairfax continued when Leah had gone, "I'm so glad you've come; it will be lovely to have a companion. It's lovely here anyway, of course – this is a fine old house, and very respectable – but it can get dreary in the wintertime, especially when one is alone. Leah's a nice girl, and John and Mary are good people, but they're servants and keep to themselves. One needs someone intelligent to talk to! You know, all last winter, I swear not a soul came to the house but the butcher and the postman with their deliveries. I felt quite cut off. The spring and summer were more pleasant, of course, and then, just recently, Adele arrived with her nurse. A child always livens up a house. And now you are here too, I'm sure I'll be quite content!"

My heart warmed as I listened to her talking of friendship and conversation. I wished with all my heart that I could be as good a friend as she hoped.

"But I'll not keep you up any longer," she said. "It's the stroke of midnight, and I'm sure you're quite exhausted. I'll show you to your room. I've given you one near to mine, at the back of the house. It's quite small, but I think you'll like it better than the big, draughty rooms at the front."

I agreed I was very tired, and we went upstairs. The upper hallway was chilly and echoing, but when Mrs. Fairfax opened the door to my room, I saw that she was right. It was small, but felt friendly and welcoming. I was too tired to stay awake any longer. I quickly unpacked my things, prepared for bed, and within minutes I was in a deep sleep.

When I awoke, it was broad daylight, and my room looked bright and pretty, as the sun shone between the blue flowered curtains onto the carpet and papered walls. It was very unlike the bare floorboards and stained plaster I was used to at Lowood. I felt as if I had entered a completely new life – one where I could look forward to happiness.

I got up and dressed, worrying about making the right impression. I didn't have any fine clothes, but I could at least make myself neat and clean. I wished, as I often had before, that I wasn't so small and plain. I longed for a nicer face – pink cheeks, a straight nose and a cherry mouth, instead of my pinched, pale looks. But I would have to do. I left my room tidy and went downstairs.

There was no one around. I walked through the hall, taking in the paintings, the bronze lamps and the grandfather clock. The front door stood half-open, so I stepped outside and across the dewy lawn into the sunshine, and looked up at the house.

It was a grand place, built of stone, with battlements at the top. Behind it was a rookery, and the rooks were flying out over the grounds, cawing and swooping in the sunshine. A row of gnarled old thorn trees divided the grounds from the meadows all around – they must have given the house its name. In the distance there were moors, and on a nearby hilltop I could see a little village with a church.

I was thinking what a fine house it was, and how big it seemed for just one old lady and a few servants, when Mrs. Fairfax appeared at the door.

"Up already?" she said. "I see you're an early riser! So, how do you like Thornfield?"

"It's lovely," I said. "I like it very much."

"Yes, it's a good house," she said. "But I'm afraid it'll fall into disrepair if Mr. Rochester doesn't look after it better. He should come here more often."

"Mr. Rochester?" I asked. "Who's he?"

"Why, the house's owner," she said. "Didn't you know he was called Rochester?"

"No – I thought the house belonged to you."

"To me? Bless you, child!" she laughed. "No, I'm just the housekeeper!"

"And the little girl – Adele, my pupil?"

"She is Mr. Rochester's ward. She's the child of someone he knew in France. Her mother abandoned her, and she's come here to live. It was Mr. Rochester who asked me to find a governess for her.

Here she comes now, with her nurse Sophie."

I turned around and saw a little girl running towards us. She was about seven years old, and very pretty, with dark hair tumbling to her waist. Her nursemaid followed behind.

"Good morning, Miss Adele," said Mrs. Fairfax. "Say hello to Miss Eyre, who is to teach you, and make you a clever lady."

"Bonjour," said Adele, and turned to her nurse, talking excitedly in French.

"Does she speak English?"

"A little, but Sophie doesn't at all. That's why I thought you would be a good teacher for her."

Now I was very glad that I had studied hard in my French lessons at Lowood, and that I had often spoken French with Madame Pierrot, as it meant I could understand what Adele was saying. As we went in to breakfast, she took my hand and began telling me all about how she had come from France with Mr. Rochester and Sophie in a big ship, which had made her seasick. She said Mr. Rochester was kind to her, but now he had gone away again.

After breakfast, I went with her to the library, where there were schoolbooks, a globe, a piano and an easel for painting and drawing, and we began her lessons. She was a bright child, and eager to please, but her mind was always wandering off this way and that. At noon, I let her finish for the day. I decided to do some drawing, and was on my way upstairs to fetch my pencils when I passed Mrs. Fairfax, dusting in the dining room.

"Your school–hours are over now, I suppose," she said. "Would you like to see the house?"

I followed her into every room, gazing in wonder at the beautiful furniture, the rich, deep carpets, and the grand, empty bedrooms with their velvet drapes and coverlets. Mrs. Fairfax dusted here and there as she showed me around.

"What good order you keep the house in," I said. "You could keep some of these rooms closed up, but you dust and clean them all."

"Well," she said, "Mr. Rochester may not come here often, but when he does, it's unexpected, and sometimes he brings visitors. He never gives us much warning. So we always keep the rooms ready."

"What is Mr. Rochester like?" I asked. I was burning with curiosity about this mystery owner.

"He's very decent," she said. "A little peculiar, perhaps, but a good man, and respected by all."

"In what way peculiar?" I asked.

"Oh... it's hard to describe," she said. "Now then. I am going up to the roof to check for dead leaves; would you like to come with me and see the view?"

We were already upstairs; now I followed her through a doorway and up a narrow staircase to the attic. We went along a gloomy passageway, then up a ladder and through a trapdoor onto the lead roof.

We were as high up as the rooks in the trees behind the house, and I could look right into their nests. Walking around the battlements, I saw the grounds laid out like a map, with the meadows, the village and the hills beyond all lying peacefully in the warm autumn sun.

By now it was almost time for lunch. While Mrs. Fairfax stayed to fasten the trapdoor, I climbed down the ladder. My eyes had grown used to the bright sunshine, and now the attic passageway seemed pitch-black. I had to feel my way along the walls in the silence.

As I was nearing the top of the attic stairs, I heard a very strange sound. It was a kind of laugh, but not a happy one. It sounded loud, hollow and inhuman

– almost like a bark. If I had been alone, and if it hadn't been the middle of the day, I would have feared it was a ghost. I hurried down the staircase and through the door into the upstairs hallway.

"Mrs. Fairfax," I called. She emerged a few moments later.

"Did you hear that strange laugh?" I asked.

"Oh, that," she said. "It's just Grace Poole."

"Who?"

"Grace Poole – didn't I mention her? She's one of the servants. She helps Leah with sewing, and some of the other chores."

Just then, I heard the laugh again, and I jumped.

"Grace!" Mrs. Fairfax called up the attic stairs.

There were footsteps on the attic staircase, and a woman appeared in the doorway. She was middle-aged and plump, with red hair and a plain, normal-looking face. You never saw a less ghostly person in your life. I could not imagine in a million years that the laugh had come from her.

"A little too much noise, Grace," said Mrs. Fairfax. Grace nodded and closed the door again, and we went down to lunch.

Rochester

I settled easily into life at Thornfield. Everyone was friendly, I had a comfortable room of my own, and I didn't have to work hard. Never before had I been granted such a pleasant existence.

And yet, ungrateful as it seems, I still felt restless, and wondered what other scenes life might hold in store. I would go up to the roof to look at the view, and as I gazed out over the hills to the horizon, I would wish I could somehow see beyond, to the places I had never been: towns, cities, regions full of life. I longed for excitement, witty conversation and new ideas. But there was nothing I could do. After a while, I would climb back down the ladder and feel my way along the dark attic passageway, letting my visions and imaginings fill my mind's eye.

When I was there, I often heard Grace Poole's laugh again – that loud, slow "Ha!" accompanied by a murmuring or scuffling sound. My heart would race and I would hurry along the passage. But whenever I saw Grace, carrying a tea tray or a pile of blankets along the hall, she always looked so normal that my fears evaporated. I would smile and say hello, but Grace Poole was not a talkative person. Hard-faced and preoccupied, she would answer with a grunt and disappear into the attic.

October, November and December passed by. Then, one day in January, Mrs. Fairfax asked if Adele could be excused, as she had a slight cold. I remembered how I had treasured time off from lessons when I was a child, and I agreed at once. We sat Adele by the fire in Mrs. Fairfax's room, with her dolls and storybooks, and I took the day off.

That afternoon, I offered to walk up to Hay, the nearby village, to post everyone's letters. I set out at three, and the winter sun was already sinking as I left the gate and turned up the lane. It was a beautiful, crisp, sharp day, with low, pale sunbeams crossing the fields. Little birds sat in the bare hawthorn hedge, like leaves that had forgotten to drop.

The road was all uphill, and after a mile or so I stopped and sat on a stile to rest. I was warm in my thick wool cloak and muffler, but it was very cold. A sheet of ice lay across the track where a little rivulet had run over it and frozen solid. From where I was sitting, I could see Thornfield, with its dark battlements and woods. Looking the other way, I saw chimney smoke rising from the houses of Hay at the top of the hill. Behind them, the moon was rising. I sat there in absolute peace, listening to the faint sound of the streams and rivers in the valley.

Just as I was about to set off again, I heard the metallic clatter of horses' hooves approaching. I couldn't see anything, as the lane was narrow and winding, but someone was certainly coming. I stood back against the stile to let them pass.

When the noise was close, but there was still no one in sight, I was startled to see a huge dog sniffing along the hedge right next to me. It was brown and white, with a long coat, and such a large, hairy head that it reminded me of a lion. I shrank back, but the dog ambled past without even looking at me. Almost at once the rider galloped past too – a man on a tall, sturdy horse – and I got up to continue my journey.

Then I heard a sliding and scraping sound, and the man cursing. I turned back to see that both horse and rider were on the ground: they had slipped on the sheet of ice I had been looking at. The dog sniffed around them, then bounded over to me, barking. I followed him back down the track.

"Are you injured, sir?" I asked. "Can I help?"

"Stand aside," the man answered gruffly, and I did so as he hauled himself upright and cajoled the horse back onto its feet, while the dog barked and leaped around manically. "Down, Pilot!" its owner shouted.

Luckily, the horse was unharmed. But the rider felt his foot and leg, then limped over to the stile where I had been sitting, and leaned on it.

"If you are hurt, sir," I said, "I can fetch someone."

"It's just a sprain, thank you," he said tersely. He tried putting his weight on the bad foot, let out a grunt of pain and sat down heavily on the stile.

It was still only dusk, and I could see him clearly. He was about thirty-five, medium in height, with broad shoulders and a stern, square, scowling face.

He had a heavy forehead, thick eyebrows and a large nose. But his gruffness and lack of beauty put me at my ease. If he had been handsome and dashing, and treated me like a lady, I would have been awkward and embarrassed. As it was, I wanted to help him.

"I cannot just leave you here, sir, unable to walk," I said. "I could fetch someone to help you get home."

"I should think you ought to be at home yourself," he said. "Where did you come from?"

"From Thornfield," I said, pointing at the house. "But I'm not afraid to be out in the dark – I'm going to Hay to post letters. I can send help from there."

"Thornfield?" he asked. "Whose house is that?"

"Mr. Rochester's."

"And who is he? Do you know him?"

"I've never met him, sir. He's not resident."

"You don't look like a servant," he remarked.

"I'm the governess," I explained.

"Aha – of course!" he said. "The governess!"

I wasn't sure how to respond, so I watched as he tried again to get up from the stile, and winced in pain. At last he said, "I will not ask you to fetch help, but perhaps you could help me to my horse."

I went over to him, and he stood up and leaned on my shoulder. With much grimacing, we reached his horse, and he hauled himself into the saddle.

"Thank you," he said. "Now, post your letters, and hurry home. Pilot!" He spurred the horse on, the dog followed, and they all disappeared down the lane.

I went on my way to Hay. The incident was over – there was no need to think about it. Yet as I walked into the village, as I posted the letters, as I tramped down the hill in the dark, I couldn't help thinking about the man. His face hung in the air before me, so stern and strong, unlike the face of anyone else I knew. When I came back past the stile, I stopped and wondered for a moment if I might meet him again. But there was no one there. I could see yellow light shining from the windows of Thornfield Hall, reminding me that I was late, and I hurried on.

When I got in, the hallway was dark, but a warm glow emanated from the dining room, whose door was half-open. I heard voices inside, including Adele's, as I walked past. I went into Mrs. Fairfax's little office. There was a fire burning in the grate, but Mrs. Fairfax was not there. Instead, I was amazed to see a large, hairy dog sitting on the hearth rug, exactly like the one I had seen in the lane. It was so similar that I called out "Pilot!", and the dog got up and bounded over to me eagerly, wagging his tail.

I was puzzled, and rang the bell to call Leah. When she came in, I asked, "Leah, who does this dog belong to?"

"Why, it's the master's dog, Pilot," she said.

"The master?"

"Yes, Mr. Rochester – he's just arrived. He's in the dining room with the others. They're calling the doctor out, since he sprained his foot on the way."

"I see," I said. I took a candle, and went upstairs to get ready for dinner.

There was no sign of Mr. Rochester that evening. The doctor must have told him to go to bed to rest his foot. I didn't see him the next morning, either, but Mrs. Fairfax told me that Adele and I must use one of the upstairs bedrooms for our lessons, as Mr. Rochester would need the library for business.

The doorbell rang constantly all day as various visitors arrived, and Adele couldn't concentrate at all. She kept running to the top of the bannisters to try to glimpse Mr. Rochester, and talking about what presents he might have for her. She said he had promised that when his luggage came from Millcote, there would be a box in it for her. She also said he had asked her all about her governess.

When our lessons were done, I let her run to the library to find him. I walked over to the window, and watched thick snowflakes falling through the air.

Mrs. Fairfax came in. "Jane," she said, "Mr. Rochester says he would like you, me and Adele to take tea with him. You'd better change your frock."

She came with me to my room and helped me to put on my evening dress, a black silk one. Onto it I pinned the only jewel I possessed, a little pearl brooch that Miss Temple had given me, and we went down to the dining room.

Mr. Rochester was resting on a sofa, with his bad foot raised up on a cushion, while Adele played with Pilot by the fire. Mrs. Fairfax introduced me to him, but he barely looked at me. While she fetched the tea, I sat down, feeling just as I had before – that his lack of courtesy made things easier for me. It meant that I felt no obligation to be polite or false myself.

"Did you bring Miss Eyre a present?" Adele cried suddenly, running over to him.

Mr. Rochester raised his eyebrows, and turned to me. "Did you expect a present, Miss Eyre?" he asked.

"I have no reason to," I said. "You hardly know me, and I have done nothing to deserve one."

"That's not true at all," he replied. "I can see what good work you have done with Adele."

"Well, sir, you have praised my work, and that is a good enough present for me," I said.

Mr. Rochester grunted, and took his cup of tea from Mrs. Fairfax.

"You have been here how long?"

"Three months, sir."

"And you came from...?"

"Lowood School, sir. I was there for eight years."

"Eight years in a place like that! Well, that explains why you have such a tough little face. You know, last night, I wondered if you had bewitched my horse, you have such an odd look in your eye."

I didn't reply.

"Who are your parents?"

"I have none."

"So when you were sitting on that stile, you were waiting for your real family, the elves and the fairies. Eh?" He was obviously testing me – provoking me, to see how I would react. But I intended to play him at his own game.

"The elves and the fairies have left England," I said calmly. "They don't live here any more. It's too modern for them."

He looked defeated for a moment. Then he began asking other questions – how I had found this job, what Lowood was like, what I thought of Mr. Brocklehurst (I told him the truth), and whether I could draw or play the piano.

At last he said, "Well, it is late: Adele must go to bed. Take her, please, Miss Eyre. Goodnight, Mrs. Fairfax," he added, to let her know that she should leave too.

"You said he was a little peculiar," I said to Mrs. Fairfax later, as we sat in front of the fire in her office. "I think he's very peculiar indeed."

"It's just his way – you'll get used to it," she said.

"But why is he like that?"

"He's had his troubles," she explained. "His brother died, you know, nine years ago, and before that he had a falling-out with his family. I think he finds it difficult to be at Thornfield."

"But nine years is long enough to settle in, surely?"

"I suppose he finds it a gloomy place," she said.

I longed to know more – something was wrong; there must be a reason he would not live here. What was it? But the look on Mrs. Fairfax's face told me I should drop the subject, and so I did.

The Fire

For the next few days I hardly saw Mr. Rochester. Most of the time he was busy with visitors and, since his sprain was better, he often went out riding. I occasionally bumped into him on the stairs or in the hall. Sometimes he would bow and smile; other times he seemed irritated, and barely glanced at me.

Then, one evening, after he had held a dinner party for some friends, he asked Mrs. Fairfax to bring Adele and me to the drawing room. His things had at last arrived from Millcote, and he presented Adele with her box of presents. While she sat on the sofa, ecstatically unwrapping little trinkets and toys, he called me to him.

"Come and be seated here, Miss Eyre," he said, pulling a chair closer to his own. "I must confess, I don't wish to spend the evening talking to a seven-year-old, sweet as she is. I would rather talk to you."

He then proceeded to stare into the fire in silence. He had placed my chair so close to him, I could do nothing but sit and look at him. His rough features and dark eyes looked softer and kinder tonight – perhaps the party had put him in a good mood.

Suddenly he turned and saw me looking at him.

"You're staring at me, Miss Eyre," he said. "Do you think I'm handsome?"

"No, sir," I said without thinking. Then I blushed furiously at how rude I had been.

Mr. Rochester laughed. "What a strange thing you are!" he said. "You seem so quiet and meek – and then, when you do speak, you're somewhat blunt!"

Yet he seemed to like this honesty in me; he was intrigued by it. He told me that I was unlike anyone else he had met, especially of so young an age, and that since I was so honest with him, he could not help but be honest with me. He said he could see that I was shy, but inside he thought I was passionate and bold. How true that was!

He also said something strange – that he had many regrets, but that he now intended to make amends and become a good person. I did not understand, but he promised to explain it to me someday. Then, suddenly, he again told me to take Adele to bed, and our conversation was over.

Not long after that, he did explain – or, at least, he told me a little about his past. It was a damp afternoon in early spring, and I had taken Adele out for some fresh air. We bumped into Mr. Rochester out walking Pilot, and while Adele played with the dog, he walked and talked with me. He told me how he had come to be looking after Adele.

It turned out that she was the daughter of a Parisian dancer, named Celine Varens. Mr. Rochester had been in love with Celine – so smitten that he had bought her jewels, expensive clothes and a carriage, and paid for her to live in a fine hotel. He had thought she loved him too. But one night, when he went to call on her unexpectedly, he was horrified to see her climbing out of her carriage with another man – a viscount whom Rochester knew well. He heard them laughing about him, and he heard Celine describe him as ugly and deformed.

Some time later, Celine ran away to Italy with her viscount. But she left her daughter behind in Paris, claiming that Rochester should look after her.

"I am not her father," Mr. Rochester explained. "And I don't know who is. But there was no one else to care for her and, as I said, I have good intentions.

"How strange that I should be telling you all this," he added, "and how odd that you listen so calmly – you are not shocked for a moment. But there is something about you – something that makes me want to confide in you." I did not reply.

"And so here she is, a little French flower, transplanted to an English country garden here at Thornfield," he continued. "And because she is here, you are here too."

He looked up at the house. "I like this house," he said, thoughtfully. "I like its worn stone, and the old thorn trees. And yet, how I've struggled to stay away, how I've hated the thought of..." He fell silent, staring up at Thornfield's windows. As I watched, I saw a range of feelings pass across his face: first a kind of impatience, then disgust and hatred, followed by guilt and pain. Finally he hardened his features into stony determination, and said, "It's time to go in."

And so Mr. Rochester became not just an absent landlord, but a friend. As time went on he became less moody, and instead always looked pleased to see me. He often wanted to talk, taking me into his confidence, and treating me almost as his equal, not as a governess, paid thirty pounds a year.

And as for me? Yes, I had called him plain – ugly, even. But his was the face I now most wanted to see. No longer did I feel isolated, cut off without interesting company. Now I had all the intelligent conversation I could wish for, and I thrived on it. I was fulfilled and happy. I laughed more, and my complexion looked brighter and healthier.

Mr. Rochester had his faults. He could be rude and harsh, moody, intolerant and sarcastic. But I felt he was a good man at heart. Whatever it was that troubled him, I wished I could soothe it.

Late that night, I lay in bed, wide awake, thinking about Mr. Rochester. I thought about the way he had looked up at the house, seeming to suffer such agony. Eight weeks had passed since he arrived; but Mrs. Fairfax had told me he hardly ever came to Thornfield for more than a fortnight. Did that mean he would have to leave soon?

Spring was nearly here, and summer and autumn lay ahead. How lonely they would be for me if he went away! What was it, I wondered, that tore at his heart, that made it so hard for him to be here?

I blew out my candle and turned over to sleep. But just as I was drifting off, I heard something that made me start awake again – a low, murmuring noise, very close by. I sat up suddenly, alert and listening. After a while, I heard the clock in the hallway strike two. Just then, it seemed that someone, or something, brushed past the door of my room.

"Who's there?" I called. Then I remembered Pilot. Perhaps the kitchen door had been left open, and he had come upstairs to look for his master. This calmed me down, and I turned over again to sleep.

"Ha!"

There it was again! That laugh – that deep, strange, unearthly laugh I had heard so many times in the attic passageway – now seemed to be right outside my door, almost as if it came in through the keyhole. In a panic I bundled myself out of bed, lunged for the door and drew the bolt across. Trembling, I called again: "Who is there?"

There was a gurgling, moaning sound, followed by footsteps moving along the hall and up the attic stairs. Could it be Grace Poole? Had she gone insane, and started wandering the house by night? I decided to wake Mrs. Fairfax, to tell her what I'd heard.

Still shaking, I pulled on a dress and a shawl, and unbolted my door. Right outside it, on the floor in front of me, stood a lighted candle in its holder. There was a strange burning smell. I looked along the hall, and suddenly realized it was full of smoke.

I ran past the candle and down the hall until I found the door the smoke was coming from. It was Mr. Rochester's. The door was ajar, and I ran in, all thoughts of Mrs. Fairfax gone from my mind. Through the smoke I saw flames darting around the curtains of the bed, and Mr. Rochester lying asleep.

"Wake up!" I shouted, running around to the side of the bed and shaking him, but he was deeply unconscious – the smoke must have dulled his senses. In a panic I rushed over to the washstand, where I found his washbasin and water jug; both were full of water and I lifted them up in turn, carried them over to the bed and drenched the curtains and blankets. The fire hissed out, and Mr. Rochester, doused with cold water, woke up, gasping and spluttering.

"Is there a flood?" he shouted through the dark.

"No, there has been a fire, sir," I called. "Stay there, and I will fetch a candle."

"Is that Jane Eyre?" he demanded. "What are you trying to do, drown me?"

I fetched the candle from outside my door. When I returned, Mr. Rochester was wearing his dressing gown. He took the candle from me and inspected the blackened, sodden bed.

"What happened?" he asked. "Who did this?"

I told him everything – how I had heard the murmur and the strange laugh, which I knew from before, and footsteps going up to the attic, and how the candle had been left outside my room.

"Should I fetch Mrs. Fairfax?" I asked.

"No – no, don't fetch anyone," he said. "Stay here in this chair, and wait for me. I am going upstairs for a minute, and I will be back soon. Don't move."

I waited there in the darkness for what seemed like hours. I was thinking about disobeying him and going back to my room when I heard him returning. He came in, looking gloomy.

"I have sorted it all out," he said. He stared at me. "You said you heard a laugh?" he asked.

"Yes, sir – an odd, low laugh."

"And you have heard it before?"

"Yes – I believe it is Grace Poole, sir, one of the servants. She laughs that way."

"That's right. It was Grace Poole. She's – well, she's a little eccentric. Now, you must promise me that you will say no more about this to anyone. I will clean up the mess; you may go back to your room."

"Goodnight then, sir."

He looked at me in dismay. "What? You are leaving me?"

"You just said I should go back to my room, sir."

"Yes, of course." He seemed confused. "But – I haven't thanked you yet. You saved my life." He put the candle down, reached out and took my hand, and held it in both of his.

"I owe you a great debt, Jane Eyre," he said, looking into my eyes. His lips moved, as if he might be about to say something else, but he did not.

"There is no debt, sir, nothing owing," I said. "I am glad I happened to be awake, and was able to help. Goodnight again, sir."

But he would not let go of my hand.

"I knew..." he said, "I knew as soon as I saw you, that you would do me good in some way." He stared at me intensely, his eyes ablaze with feeling.

"I think I hear Mrs. Fairfax stirring, sir," I said.

"Well, then you must go," he said, releasing me.

Back in my bed, I could not sleep for a second. My brain turned over and over the strange and dramatic events of the night, until I was exhausted. Feelings of terror, when I thought of what might have happened, constantly changed places with joy, when I thought of the touch of his hand, and the look I had seen in his eyes.

Blanche Ingram

The next day, I heard Mrs. Fairfax and the servants talking about the fire as if it had been nothing but an accident, which Mr. Rochester himself had dealt with.

"What a blessing he was not burned in his bed!" they exclaimed. "It is always dangerous to keep a candle lit at night." "It's a mercy he thought of using the water jug."

When I walked past Mr. Rochester's room, I saw that everything had been cleaned up. The charred curtains were gone from the bed, and Leah was busy scrubbing the smoke-stained window panes.

I was about to go in and speak to her, when I saw someone else sitting in the room. It was Grace Poole. She was sewing new bed curtains, and looked as plain and poker-faced as ever. How could she still be here, after what she had done last night? I was sure she would have been dismissed immediately. I stepped into the room.

"Good morning, Grace," I said. "What happened here? I heard the others talking about a fire..."

"Indeed Miss, last night the master fell asleep with his candle lit, and the curtains caught fire; but he woke and quenched the flames with the water jug."

There was not a hint of guilt in her face.

"It's a wonder no one heard anything," I said. "Didn't he wake anyone?"

"The servants sleep so far off," said Grace, concentrating on her sewing. "Only you and Mrs. Fairfax sleep near this room, and she is an old lady and sleeps soundly. Why, did you hear something, Miss?" With this she looked up at me, and at last I thought I could see awareness behind her eyes.

"I did," I said, "but I thought it was just Pilot. But then... Pilot does not laugh, does he? I heard a laugh."

Grace took another piece of thread and threaded her needle purposefully. "I hardly think the master would laugh, Miss, when he was in such danger," she remarked. "Perhaps you were dreaming."

"I was not," I said, rather indignantly.

She stared at me. "So what did you do?" she asked.

"I bolted my door," I replied.

"You do not bolt it every night, as a habit?"

"No."

"Well," said Grace enigmatically. "You should." She looked down, and our conversation was over.

For the rest of the day I puzzled over this mystery. What strange hold did Grace Poole have over Mr. Rochester? She had tried to murder him – he had told me as much last night – yet he had chosen to cover up her crime, and seemed to have no intention of getting rid of her.

I longed to see him, so I could ask him what was going on. We knew each other well enough by now, and I was sure I could raise the matter without offending him. But there was no sign of him. I asked Mrs. Fairfax where he was.

"Oh, Mr. Rochester is gone to visit friends on the other side of Millcote," she said. "They are having quite a party."

"Is he expected back tonight?"

"No, nor tomorrow either – I should think he will stay a week or more. He's very popular among his friends, you know – especially the ladies."

I felt a chill around my heart, but I composed myself while Mrs. Fairfax rattled on: "One might not think him the best-looking of gentlemen, I suppose, but perhaps it is his wealth and his accomplishments that make the ladies like him."

"Are there ladies at this party?" I asked.

"Oh, of course – Mrs. Eshton, and her three daughters, and Maria and Blanche Ingram – Blanche is the most beautiful of them all. I saw her when she came to a Christmas ball here, some years ago – why, the room fairly lit up when she walked in."

"What is she like?"

"Tall and shapely, with lovely olive skin, and dark eyes, so sparkling they are, like jewels, and the thickest, glossiest black hair you ever saw, all in curls and ringlets. On that night, she was wearing a white gown and an amber scarf – how perfect she looked! She and Mr. Rochester sang a duet, I remember."

"Mr. Rochester can sing?" I asked, trying to sound

as calm as I could.

"Yes, he has a fine voice, like Miss Blanche."

"How nice," I smiled.

Alone in my room that night, I berated myself for ever thinking Mr. Rochester could like me. A few kind words, a chance look in his eye in a dark room filled with smoke – and I had dared to imagine he had feelings for me. Well, he did not. Why should he, when there were women like Blanche Ingram in his world – beautiful, accomplished, and of his own class? He would never choose me over someone like her. I had to stop dreaming.

I forced myself to look in the mirror at my plain little face, my thin lips, sallow skin and flat brown hair. I resolved to paint two pictures – one of myself, just as I was, and one of Blanche Ingram, beautiful and glowing, just as Mrs. Fairfax had described her. Then, whenever I felt a twinge of feeling for Mr. Rochester, I would look at the pictures to remind myself just how stupid I was being.

A week went by, and I tried to forget my disappointment. I worked hard with Adele, and busied myself with my painting and sewing. When Mrs. Fairfax declared she didn't know when Mr. Rochester would return, and that he might be gone for a year for all she knew, I told myself it was no business of mine.

Yet when, two weeks after Mr. Rochester had gone, Mrs. Fairfax received a letter from him, I could hardly keep myself from trembling as she read it through.

"Well," she said, "I often say Thornfield is too quiet, but we'll be busy enough now, that's for sure."

"What does the letter say?" I asked, trying to sound unconcerned.

"The master's coming back on Thursday, and he's bringing his friends with him," she said. "He wants all the bedrooms made up, and I'm to bring in extra kitchen staff. What with all the lords and ladies and their maids and valets, we'll have a full house!"

The next three days were taken up with preparing the house. Beds were aired, carpets were beaten, fireplaces were swept, and vases were filled with flowers. Extra servants were employed from the village, and I had to help too, so Adele was excused from her lessons. She ran around the house in a frenzy of excitement, bouncing on the beds and chattering as we dusted, scrubbed and polished.

One afternoon, in the midst of all this activity, I heard Leah talking to one of the extra servants about Grace Poole, and I stopped to eavesdrop.

"She's paid well, I suppose?" said the girl.

"Oh, yes," said Leah. "Five times what I get, and that's generous enough. Still, she deserves it — there's few could do what she does, for any money."

I did not see what was so challenging about sewing curtains and tablecloths, which seemed to be Grace Poole's main task.

"I wonder whether the master — "

"Shhh," said Leah. She had spotted me nearby.

"Doesn't she know?" the girl whispered. Leah shook her head, and continued dusting in silence.

Thursday arrived, and Mrs. Fairfax dressed in her best silk frock, with ladylike gloves and a gold watch. Adele too put on her best dress. But I saw no reason why I should – I would not be needed, after all.

"They were supposed to be here at six," tutted Mrs. Fairfax, coming into the upstairs schoolroom where Adele and I were sitting and reading. "I'm glad I asked for dinner to be prepared late!"

"They're coming," called John from downstairs. He had ridden out to the gates to look down the lane towards Millcote. "They'll be here in ten minutes!"

Adele rushed to the window, and we joined her.

I stood to one side, so that I couldn't be seen from the drive. Adele hopped and danced on the spot, bursting with anticipation, until at last we heard horses' hooves. Four riders galloped up the drive, followed by two open carriages filled with gentlemen and ladies. Two of those on horseback were handsome young men. In front of them rode Mr. Rochester, with Pilot bounding along behind; and beside him rode a stunningly beautiful lady. Her long purple riding cloak almost swept the ground, and thick, glossy, raven-black curls tumbled about her neck.

"Miss Ingram!" exclaimed Mrs. Fairfax, and she hurried away to greet the guests downstairs.

Adele longed to meet the visitors, but that evening it was not to be. I found a cold chicken and some bread in the larder, which Adele, Sophie and I shared for our supper. Meanwhile, the guests enjoyed a long and lavish dinner in the dining room. It was past one in the morning when they went to bed, and Adele had long since fallen asleep.

The next day, Mrs. Fairfax and I again watched from the window as the party returned from riding. Again, Mr. Rochester and Blanche rode together, and I remarked that they seemed close.

"Yes, I'm sure he admires her," Mrs. Fairfax said.

"She is very beautiful," I agreed.

"Well, you'll meet her tonight," she said. "I told Mr. Rochester how excited Adele was, and he said you must bring her to the drawing room this evening."

My heart felt heavy as I put on my dull dress and my tiny brooch, and tried to smooth down my hair. We waited in the drawing room while the guests ate, and passed the time by choosing a flower from one of the many overflowing vases around the room, and fixing it to the sash of Adele's pink satin frock.

At last the door from the dining room opened, and the ladies came in. There were only eight of them, but with their bright silk dresses, fringed shawls and waving feather plumes, they seemed to fill the room. I curtsied politely as they entered, and one or two of them nodded; the rest ignored me.

Adele wasted no time in making new friends. She introduced herself in French; and soon half of the ladies were cooing around her, admiring her dress and exclaiming over how sweet she was.

Meanwhile, I seated myself in the shadowiest corner I could find, hoping to get a good look at Blanche without her seeing me. Could she really be so perfect? And – I couldn't stop myself from thinking it – did Mr. Rochester really like her?

She was without doubt the most beautiful woman in the room. Tall and straight as a poplar tree, her neck and shoulders were slender and graceful, and her large, dark eyes glinted brightly in the candlelight. But there was something haughty about her. She had a proud look, and a sarcastic sneer on her cherry-red lips.

Coffee was served, and the gentlemen came in. Now I would see Mr. Rochester and Blanche together, and find out what I really wanted to know.

As Mr. Rochester went over to a group of the ladies and began talking to them, I couldn't help staring at him. Seeing him again made me think of the last time we had been together – that night after the fire, in his room, when he had held me by the hand. The handsome looks and charming smiles of the gentlemen around him seemed meaningless to me. I cared only for Mr. Rochester's rough features, his heavy brow and intelligent glance.

I never meant to love him, and I had tried to stop. But it was useless. I knew I must hide my feelings, but I could no longer tell myself they didn't exist.

Now the coffee was handed around, and everyone sat down. Only Mr. Rochester still stood, leaning on the fireplace, and soon Blanche went over to join him. I was close enough to hear what they said.

"I thought you didn't care for children," she teased.

"I don't, not really," he replied.

"Then why do you keep that little thing?" she said rudely, pointing at Adele. "Where did you get her?"

"She was left for me to look after."

"You could at least send her away to school," Blanche said. "Then you wouldn't need to pay for a governess – or have to house and feed them both."

"I hadn't thought about it," said Mr. Rochester.

"No – you men never do," she laughed. "But, the truth is, governesses are generally a nuisance – at least, Maria and I never had a nice one. Did we, Mama?"

At this, Blanche's mother, Lady Ingram,

exclaimed, "Heavens, don't talk to me about governesses! Thank goodness I no longer have to employ them, now my girls are grown."

Another, kinder-looking lady leaned over and said something quietly to Lady Ingram. Perhaps she was reminding her that a governess was in the room.

"Who cares?" the older woman snorted. And so the conversation continued, with several of the guests joining in to make rude remarks about governesses they had employed in the past, until Blanche decided it was time for some music.

"Edward, I hope you are in fine voice tonight," she called flirtatiously, as she made her way to the piano.

"If you wish it, I will be," smiled Mr. Rochester.

"Well, then, I do," giggled Blanche, and she sat down and began to play – very well, I had to admit.

I decided that this was a good time to make my getaway. I was just about to slip unnoticed out of a side-door, when Mr. Rochester began to sing. His voice was beautiful – a deep, mellow bass – and he sang with great emotion. I stayed to listen until the end of the song, soaking up the warmth and feeling of every note. Then, just as the chattering began again, I left.

I noticed my sandal was loose, and stopped in the hall to retie it. As I was kneeling down, I heard footsteps. Someone had followed me. I stood up and turned, and came face to face with Mr. Rochester.

"Jane, how are you?" he said.

"I am very well."

"Why did you not come and talk to me in there?"

I might as well have asked him the same question.

"I could see how busy you were," I said at last.

"You look pale," he said. "Is anything wrong?"

"No, nothing is wrong," I said, but I could feel tears behind my eyes.

"You're upset about something," he said.

"No – really..."

"Yes, you are, and if I had time I would find out what. As it is, I must ask you to send Sophie down to take Adele to bed, and bid you goodnight. But I want you to join us in the drawing room tomorrow night, and every night, Jane. Do you understand?"

I looked up at him, and a tear rolled down my cheek and splashed onto the floor.

He took my hand again, as he had done after the fire. "Goodnight, my – " He stopped, bit his lip, and went back into the drawing room.

The Gypsy

How different Thornfield seemed, now it was no longer empty and quiet! The house was full of life and activity. You could not enter a room or climb the stairs without bumping into a neatly dressed lady's maid or gentleman's valet.

The guests spent their time walking in the gardens, having picnics on the lawn, or chattering and laughing in the drawing room. In the evenings, they often played charades. They hung a curtain over a doorway, and turned it into a miniature stage, on which words and phrases were acted out.

On these occasions I had to endure the sight of Blanche Ingram flirting with Mr. Rochester as they took their parts. In one charade, they even enacted a wedding scene, with her as the bride and him as the groom. Seeing this stung me to my heart.

I loved Mr. Rochester deeply, and I could not stop loving him, just because another woman now came first in his affections. I knew they would probably marry soon, and if Blanche had been worthy of him, I would have accepted that.

But she was not worthy of him. Oh, yes, she was tall, beautiful and accomplished. But she was empty-headed. She had nothing to say. All her fine ways were calculated and cold, and she had no true tenderness or sympathy. I saw her being impatient with Adele. I heard her make hurtful remarks, and repeat witty phrases which I knew were from books. I saw the snooty looks she gave me, and even the other ladies.

I was convinced Mr. Rochester saw all this too, for he watched her as carefully as I did. It was clear he didn't love her. They were not really intimate; I was sure he didn't confide in her, as he had in me.

No – if he meant to marry her, it was for appearances, and family connections. That was what wealthy people did, and who was I to blame them? I reminded myself that he was free to make his own choice, even if I did not agree with it.

One day, Mr. Rochester was called to Millcote on business. It was a rainy day, and the guests settled down to read or play cards in the drawing room.

When a carriage pulled up outside, everyone thought it was the master coming home. But it was a tall, anxious-looking stranger who was shown into the hall. He introduced himself as Mr. Mason, an old friend of Mr. Rochester's.

"I'm sorry to arrive when Mr. Rochester is away," I heard him tell Mrs. Fairfax, "but I have had a long journey, and I must wait here until he returns."

Mr. Mason joined us in the drawing room, where he talked to some of the gentlemen. Listening to them, I gathered that he lived abroad, in the West

Indies, and that he had met Mr. Rochester there.

Just as I was wondering why Mr. Rochester might have gone to such a faraway place, a footman came in. He said that an old gypsy woman had come to the house. She was refusing to leave until she had told the fortunes of all the single ladies present.

"Send her away at once!" snapped Lady Ingram. "Surely we do not want a low-bred gypsy in here?"

"But, Mama," Blanche interrupted, "I want to hear my fortune." The others agreed, and after some arguing, they agreed to let the gypsy wait in the library, where they could consult her one by one.

Blanche went in first, followed by her sister Maria, and Amy and Louisa Eshton. When Blanche came back, she seemed annoyed, but the other girls couldn't stop giggling and exclaiming over the gypsy's hideous, strange appearance, and the uncanny things she had said. She had seemed to know everything about them – all about their childhoods, their families, their hopes and fears.

Then the footman returned, and said that although she had been well paid, the gypsy woman still would not go.

"She says there is another unmarried young lady here, whom she wishes to speak to," he said. He looked at me. "Miss Eyre, she must mean you."

By now I was intrigued by what the others had said, and longed to know more about the old woman's skills. So I got up eagerly and went to the library.

When I went in, the gypsy was sitting in an

armchair in the corner of the room. She wore a red cloak and a broad hat, with a handkerchief tied under her chin. I could not see much of her face, but when she glanced up at me, I could see that she was indeed very ugly. She had thick, heavy features, and tufts of coarse hair on her cheeks.

"Well, and do you want your fortune told?" she asked, in a squeaky, rasping voice.

"I don't mind, but if you would like to tell it, do."

"That answer is typical of you," she croaked. "You pretend you don't care about things, but you do. You have secret desires and hopes. Don't you, my dear?"

I smiled. "Perhaps."

"Of course you do. And you can have the happiness you seek – it's waiting for you – but you must reach for it, you must take it for yourself."

"Since you can see the future," I said, "perhaps you can answer me this. Is Mr. Rochester to be married?"

"Ah yes," she said excitedly, "to the beautiful Miss Ingram. But he doesn't have as much money as she thought. I told her that half an hour since, and her face fell. If she finds a richer man, she'll drop him."

"And what about me?" I said. "What does my future hold?"

"Let me look at your face, and I will read it," she said, more gently, and I knelt down on the rug before her. She looked at me closely.

"There's much to read here," she said, turning my cheek in her rough hand. "An eye that flickers with fire, and sees clearly. A mouth that speaks what the brain conceives, but hides what the heart feels. It should smile more often. And a forehead, firm and calm, that speaks of reason and common sense. Whatever passions may burn within you, good judgement shall always have the last word."

She was silent for a moment. "And that is how it shall be," she said at last. "I must ignore passion, and stick to my plans. You do think I am doing the right thing, don't you, Jane, in getting married?"

I stared at the gypsy in amazement. The voice had changed — it was much deeper and more relaxed.

Then Mr. Rochester reached up and pulled the hat and hankerchief from his face. I stared in shock.

"Can you forgive me, Jane?" he asked. He held out his hand again — how could I not have recognized it before? I saw, now, the ring he wore on his little finger — a ring I had seen a hundred times.

I got up and stepped away. "I don't know," I said. I was racking my brains, wondering if I had embarrassed myself by anything I had said.

"Please, Jane," he pleaded. "It was wrong of me. You have nothing to be ashamed of." It was as if he really could read my mind. "I just wanted to know what... what did the others think? What did they say?"

But I was still in a state of shock. "I had better go," I said hastily. "Dinner will be ready." Then I suddenly remembered Mr. Mason. "Oh — sir," I added. "Did you know that you have a new visitor? A Mr. Mason, from the West Indies."

Mr. Rochester flinched as if he had been stung.

His face froze, and he became as pale as a ghost.

"Mason..." he said under his breath. "Mason!"

"Sir?" I said, coming back to him. "Are you well? Can I do anything to help?"

"Yes," he said, rubbing his face with his hands, and turning this way and that, like a man in despair. "Please go and find the others – they will be dining – and tell Mr. Mason I am back and will see him now, here in the library." He took off the cloak to reveal his usual clothes, and trembled as he threw it aside. "Bring him here, as soon as you can, Jane."

I did so, and then, when I had eaten my dinner, I went to my room. Some time later, as I lay in bed, I heard Mr. Rochester leading Mr. Mason along the hallway, and showing him to a chamber that had been prepared for him. Their voices sounded cheery, and it seemed there was nothing to worry about. I turned over, and soon fell soundly asleep.

I had left my curtains open, and when the moon, which was full that night, came around to the back of the house, it shone right into my room and woke me up. I climbed out of bed and went to the window, pausing for a moment in the still silence to admire the moon's perfect, pale face in the sky. Then I lifted my hand to pull the curtains closed.

Suddenly, a terrible, savage scream ripped the night apart. It echoed the length of Thornfield Hall, then died away, leaving me fixed to the spot, my arm half-raised and trembling.

The scream had come from above and, sure

enough, as I listened, I heard the sounds of a struggle in an attic room upstairs. Then a muffled man's voice shouted: "Help! Help! Help!"

There was a scuffling, staggering noise, and the man cried again: "Rochester! For God's sake, come!"

I heard Mr. Rochester's door opening, and his footsteps running up to the attic. From above, there was a thud, and then silence.

Horror flooded through me, but I pulled on a dress as quickly as I could, and opened the door of my room. I was not alone. The hallway was filling up with confused, startled guests in nightgowns, blinking in the moonlight and all talking at once: "What happened?"; "What on Earth was that noise?"; "Fetch a candle!"; "Where the devil is Rochester?"

"I'm here." Mr. Rochester emerged from the attic staircase, a candle in his hand. "Don't panic. A servant has had a nightmare, that is all. Please go back to bed; everything is under control."

I went back into my room, but not to sleep. I waited, fully dressed, by my window, looking out over the silvery moonlit fields and trees. What I was waiting for, I did not know. But, soon enough, the call came.

A hand tapped gently at my door, and Mr. Rochester's voice whispered: "Jane... are you up?"

I opened the door. "I am here," I said.

"Bring a sponge and a basin of water, and follow me," he said. "We must make no noise."

I did as I was told, and he led me up the attic stairs, along the dark passageway and through a door.

Inside, I saw a large bed, its curtains pulled shut. A tapestry on the wall had been drawn back to reveal another, smaller door, which was open. From beyond it, I heard, at close hand, that gurgling, snarling laugh, ending in the long, low "Ha!" that had so often terrified me before.

So Grace Poole was there. This must be where she slept.

Mr. Rochester went into the second room, and I heard him speaking in a low voice. He returned, closing the door firmly. Then he led me around the bed, and pulled the curtain aside to reveal Mr. Mason, fully dressed and lying back awkwardly, his face pale and anguished. One of his shirt sleeves, and the bedlinen around it, was soaked in blood.

"Don't worry, Richard, the wound is not serious," Rochester told Mr. Mason. "I will fetch a surgeon, and Jane here will look after you while I am gone. Jane, I want you to sponge the blood, and give Mr. Mason water if he feels faint. But you are not to speak to him – and Richard, you are not to speak to her, on pain of your life. I will be back soon."

How endless that night seemed! Hour after hour I mopped the blood and wrung out the sponge, and cooled the poor man's brow, all the time in a state of terror that Grace Poole, that mysterious murderess, would break out of her little room and attack me. We both obeyed Mr. Rochester and spoke not a word to each other; but when at last he came back, with the doctor at his side, their conversation told me more about what had happened.

"This is not just a knife wound," said the doctor. "There are tooth marks here."

"She bit me," Mason gasped. "When Rochester got the knife off her, she attacked me like a tigress..."

"I did warn you," said Mr. Rochester. "Now, man, hurry up with that bandaging," he told the doctor. He sent me to fetch Mr. Mason a clean shirt, and within half an hour, the doctor was gone, and the visitor had been bundled into a carriage and whisked away, before the sun or the servants rose.

After helping Mason into his carriage, Mr. Rochester and I stood alone in front of the house.

"Come and walk with me, Jane," he said. We wandered along a walkway in the garden, bordered with flowers. He picked a rose and gave it to me.

"Again, I must say thank you, Jane," he said. "You have had a difficult night. Were you afraid?"

"I was afraid Grace Poole would get out and attack me, sir," I admitted. "It seems to me it is not safe while she is here. I do not understand why you don't send her away."

"Don't worry about her," he said. "I can take care of the situation. Jane..." he said, and took my hand again, squeezing it tightly. "What cold fingers. Jane, when will we be together like this again?"

"I will come whenever you need me, sir."

"Then..." he seemed to be about to say something, but changed his mind. At last he said: "Perhaps you will spend some time with me the night before I get married, and talk to me," he said at last. "I'm sure I shall not be able to sleep."

Gateshead Hall

That same afternoon, Mrs. Fairfax called me to the servants' entrance, where a visitor was waiting for me. He was dressed in black, with a black band around his hat – the sign of mourning.

"My name is Robert Leaven, Miss," he said. "Coachman at Gateshead Hall. I married Bessie Lee."

"At Gateshead?!" I gasped. "Well – how do you do? How is Bessie? And why have you come all this way?"

"Bessie is very well, thank you, Miss – she has just had another baby. We have three children now."

"And the Reed family – are they well?"

"It's not such good news about them," he said, looking down at the hat in his hand. "John Reed died, just a week since, at his offices in London."

"No! What happened?"

"He was leading a wild life, Miss – drinking, and gambling, and using up all his mother's money. He was always being tricked and fooled by the rogues he knew. He came to his mother just this month, to ask for more funds, but she said no. The next we knew, he was dead. They say he killed himself."

"That is terrible! How is his mother taking it?"

"Very bad, Miss. The news brought on a stroke, and now I fear she's close to death herself. She didn't speak for three days, but when she could, she called for you. 'Bring Jane, fetch Jane Eyre,' she says; 'I must speak to her'. She won't stop asking for you."

"Well then, I must come," I said. "I'll have a room made up for you, and we'll leave in the morning."

I found Mr. Rochester in the billiard room, playing a game with Blanche. She looked down her nose at me as I approached, but it could not wait.

"Mr. Rochester," I said. "I must speak to you."

He turned and saw me, laid down his cue and followed me outside.

"I must beg leave for a week or two, sir," I said.

"What for? To go where?"

"To see a lady who is very sick, sir."

"Who? You don't know any ladies."

"Mrs. Reed of Gateshead Hall, sir. She is my aunt."

"But you said you had no family."

"They disowned me, sir – but now Mrs. Reed is dying, and I must go to her."

He seemed annoyed. "Very well," he said in the end, "but you must promise me you'll only stay a week, no more."

"Thank you, sir. And there is one more thing."

"What's that?"

"I must remind you, sir, if you are to be married to Blanche, Adele will have to go away to school, so she does not get in the new Mrs. Rochester's way.

And that means I will not have a job. I mean to advertize soon, for a new position."

He looked horrified. "No!" he said at first, then: "No... you must not advertize. Leave it to me. I will find you a new position."

After a two-day journey, we arrived at the lodge of Gateshead Hall on a warm spring afternoon.

"Bless you, Jane! I knew you would come! Oh, you've grown into quite a lady!" Bessie was in the doorway, with a baby in her arms. Behind her, two more children played by the hearth. "This is young Robert, and my little girl Jane," she said.

As I watched her bustling about, setting out the tea things and cutting slices of bread, old memories crowded my mind. Bessie was still only in her twenties, and as sweet and pretty as ever. But what would it be like seeing Mrs. Reed?

"I hope I'm not too late," I said. "Is Mrs. Reed still alive?"

"Oh yes," said Bessie. "She was a little better today, and still asking for you, all this morning. We'll go and see her after we've had some tea."

As we walked up the drive from the lodge to the house, I remembered the last time I had been here, nine years ago now, when Bessie took me out to catch the coach that would take me to Lowood. Then I had been angry and full of hatred – and, even now, it was hard not to feel a sense of misery as I stared up at the familiar windows.

I went into the breakfast room first, and there,

sitting at the table, were Georgiana and Eliza Reed.

I hardly recognized them at first. Eliza was tall and thin, with combed-back hair, a crucifix around her neck, and a severe expression on her face. Georgiana, by contrast, had grown very plump, though she still had her yellow ringlets and pretty blue eyes. They both wore black. But, while Eliza's dress was straight and plain, Georgiana's was of fashionable ruffled silk.

They rose and greeted me politely as "Miss Eyre", but I could see the distrust in their eyes. When I asked to see Mrs. Reed, Georgiana looked shocked.

"Oh no, Mama is too sick for visitors," she said.

"I know she asked especially to see me," I said.

"She doesn't want to be disturbed," said Eliza.

But these two had power over me no longer, and I did not intend to have a wasted journey. So I went to the housekeeper, and told her I would be staying for several days. Then I found Bessie, and asked her to take me to see Mrs. Reed.

We knocked quietly and entered Mrs. Reed's room. How often had I been summoned there as a child, to be scolded for crimes I had not committed! But when I saw Mrs. Reed, I felt only pity for her.

She was lying in her bed, her round, stern face pale and gaunt, and her eyes, watery and confused, gazed up at us. I went over and sat beside her.

"You are Jane Eyre," she said quietly.

"Yes, aunt," I said, and took her hand. But she pulled it away, and a change came over her face.

"Jane Eyre," she said again, more angrily. "Heaven knows the trouble I had with that girl! No child was ever so contrary – an unnatural little fiend, she was!"

"Why did you hate her so much?" I asked gently.

"I hated her mother – she was my husband's only sister, and I swear he put her before me, his own wife! When we heard she was dead, oh, of course, he had to send for the baby. And then he made me vow to care for the little brat when he died! He was a weak man, Reed – not like my son John – no, he's a Gibson through and through. But if only he'd stop asking me for money! Oh, John! I dreamed about him – I saw him with a wound in his throat..."

"She is confused, Miss, she's rambling," said Bessie. "We had better leave."

It was several days before Mrs. Reed recovered. I spent most of my time drawing. Eliza read, sewed or wrote letters, while Georgiana sighed with boredom, declaring how she longed to go to London. They both seemed impatient for their mother to die, and they didn't like each other's company either.

One day, when everyone was busy, I decided to go up to Mrs. Reed's room on my own, to see if she was well enough to talk to me again.

"Aunt Reed?" I called, pushing open her door. I went over to her.

"It is Jane Eyre, is it not?" she asked weakly. Her eyes looked hollow, but she was awake.

"Yes, aunt Reed. I heard you wanted to talk to me."

She stared at me for a while. Then at last she said: "I am very ill, I know. And I must ease my mind before I die. Are we alone?" I assured her we were.

"Then I must tell you, Jane Eyre, that I have done you two wrongs. Firstly, I broke my promise to my husband, that I would bring you up as my own child. And secondly... Jane, go to my dressing table, open the drawer, and take out the letter you see there."

When I held the letter in my hand, she said, "You may read it," and I did so.

> *Madam,*
>
> *I write to ask you to send me the address of my niece, Jane Eyre. Fate has blessed me with a good fortune and, as I am unmarried, Miss Eyre is my closest relative. I would now like to adopt her, and bring her to live with me here, and bequeath her whatever I have when I die.*
>
> *Yours truly,*
> *John Eyre, Madeira.*

The letter was dated three years previously.

"Mrs. Reed," I said calmly, although my heart was pounding. "This letter is three years old. Why did you not send it to me?"

She looked away. "Because I hated you – I could not forget how you had spoken to me, and what a little wretch you were. So I wrote to him, and told him you had died at Lowood, of the typhus."

I returned to her side. "Forgive me, aunt, for my rudeness — for I was just a child — and I will forgive you." I leaned down to kiss her. But she turned away.

"You may write to him now," she groaned. "You may tell him the truth. Now leave me."

"You have my forgiveness, aunt," I said, folding the letter in my hand. She said nothing.

The next morning, we found that she had died in the night.

The funeral was arranged, and held a week later. After that, the sisters begged me to stay a little longer, while they sorted through their mother's things — because, I suppose, they could hardly bear to be alone together. In the end, a month, not a week, had passed when I finally set off home to Thornfield.

I say home, for Thornfield was my home now. But for how long? Mrs. Fairfax had written to me at Gateshead to tell me that the visitors were gone, and that Mr. Rochester had been to London to buy a new carriage for his wedding. He would be married very soon. And what would I do then?

When I reached Millcote, I left my suitcase at the inn to be delivered, and walked the last few miles to Thornfield. It was a hot June day, and the haymakers were at work. As I neared the house I began to feel happy, because I knew I would soon see Mr. Rochester again. Though I was about to be parted from him, I resolved to treasure our time together — even if it was just a few days.

I came up the lane, past the rose hedges and the tall briar bush. Then I saw Mr. Rochester, sitting on a stone stile that I had been planning to climb over.

"Hello!" he called. "There you are! Where have you been all this time?"

"With my aunt, sir."

"Absent from home a whole month — and I told you to stay no more than a week! I'll swear you've quite forgotten me!"

"No sir, of course not," I said, blushing. Inside, my heart swelled with joy, that he should care whether I forgot him or not. I decided to change the subject.

"Mrs. Fairfax tells me you have a new carriage."

"I do, Jane! You must come and see it soon, and tell me if you think it will suit my bride." Then he stood up to let me pass. "Now go home, and rest."

I meant to go back to the house without another word. But, after I had crossed the stile, a strange courage took hold of me, and I turned to face him.

"Thank you, sir," I said, "for your kindness. I am so glad to see you again. I feel as if wherever you are is my true home."

Then I ran up to the house as fast as I could.

A Proposal

That night was midsummer's eve, and I went walking in the orchard at dusk. The air was warm, and the scent of flowers and the sweet song of the nightingale surrounded me. I felt I could wander there forever.

As I came around a corner, I saw Mr. Rochester. He was leaning over, peering closely at something. I thought he hadn't seen me, but he called: "Look at this moth, Jane. It's so big, it reminds me of the insects I used to see in the West Indies."

I joined him, and we walked down to the great old horse chestnut tree at the bottom of the orchard.

"Will you miss Thornfield, Jane?" he asked.

"Of course," I said quietly. "Must I leave soon?"

"I'm afraid so," he said. "It is all arranged. I hope to be a bridegroom within a month, and I have found a job for you – with a Mrs. O'Gall, in Ireland."

"Ireland? That is a long way away, sir!"

"From what?"

"From Thornfield... from England..." I could feel myself starting to cry. "From you, sir."

"If you go to Ireland, Jane, you know we will never meet again."

At this, I could hold in my grief no longer. I burst into tears, and sobbed helplessly.

"Indeed," he said, "perhaps you should not go..." He was silent for a moment. Then he said: "Because I have a strange feeling about you, Jane — as if your heart is tied to mine, under our ribs, with an invisible string. And if you went to Ireland, I'm afraid the string would break, and my heart would bleed, and you would forget about me."

I looked up at him, no longer trying to hide my tearstained face. "I would never forget you," I said. "My life here has had everything I could ever wish for — comfort, kindness and, in you, a true companion. When I think about leaving, it is like thinking about dying."

"Then don't leave," he said.

"I have to leave," I sobbed. "I cannot bear to, but nor can I bear to stay here, to become nothing to you. Do you think I can tolerate seeing you with a wife you do not love? Do you think I have no feelings? Do you think, because I am poor and plain, that I have no soul? Well, you are wrong! I have just as much soul as you — my feelings are just as strong as yours!" I shouted, gasping for breath. But, before I could go on, he grabbed my arm, pulled me towards him, and kissed my face. I struggled and pulled away.

"Don't leave," he said. "Stay, Jane, stay with me."

"I must go!" I cried. "I cannot watch you marry her."

"Then I will marry you," he said.

"What? You are tormenting me!" I cried.

A Proposal

"No. I will have no bride but you, Jane. I am not going to marry Miss Ingram."

"But – why not?"

"Well, as you so rightly say, I don't love her. Furthermore, she doesn't love me. After I told her, disguised as the gypsy, that my fortune was just a third of what it really is, she was nothing but rude to me. I have known for a long time that I do not want to marry her. The carriage, the preparations – they are for you. I love you, Jane. Please say yes."

I looked into his face, and saw that he was not teasing me. He meant it.

"Then, sir, the answer is yes," I said at last.

"Call me Edward – call me by my name."

"Yes, Edward, I will marry you!" I said.

A Proposal

And we embraced tightly and kissed, as the first drops of a rainstorm began to fall around us.

We went inside, arm in arm, and Mr. Rochester kissed me again to bid me goodnight before I went up to my room. I saw Mrs. Fairfax staring at us in amazement, but I decided I would explain later.

When I awoke the next morning, before I got up, Adele burst into my room to tell me that the great horse chestnut in the orchard had been struck by lightning, and had split in two.

As I got dressed, I wondered if I had imagined or dreamed the events of the night before. Was I really to be married? I wouldn't let myself believe it until I saw Mr. Rochester, and heard him tell me so again.

I put on my most summery dress, and looked in the mirror. My face was rosy and smiling, and the dress seemed to fit me better than it ever had before. I felt beautiful.

I ran downstairs and out into the garden. The storm had disappeared, giving way to a fine midsummer morning, with the promise of a hot day.

Mrs. Fairfax came out to call me to breakfast, and I was surprised at how grave and gloomy she looked. I wanted to wait until I had seen Mr. Rochester before telling her the news, so I said nothing. We ate in silence, and it was clear Mrs. Fairfax was not in a good mood.

After breakfast, I went straight to the schoolroom to begin Adele's lessons. But before I could go in, Adele came running gleefully out of the room to tell me that Mr. Rochester had given her the day off.

I went in, and saw him standing there.

"Jane." he beamed. "You look truly pretty today." He hugged and kissed me, and I knew it was true.

"Just a month from today," he said into my ear, "You will become Mrs. Jane Rochester. This very morning I have written to my bank in London, asking them to send the Rochester family jewels from their vault – diamonds and gold for me to hang around your neck. And I will buy you beautiful dresses of satin and lace – "

"Stop," I interrupted him. "Please, stop talking like this. It isn't right. If you dress me up in these fripperies, I will not be myself. I am not a society lady, sir, you know that. I am just a governess."

But he hushed me, and went on: "Today, Jane, we will go in the new carriage to Millcote; and you will choose some new clothes. We will be married in just four weeks, at eight in the morning, and you must have a wedding dress. And, as soon as we are married, we will set off for London, and go from there to France and Italy, for our honeymoon. You will need clothes and other things for the journey."

"I am to travel?" I asked, amazed. "To France, and Italy?"

"Of course, my love," he said. "I will show you the world, and take you to see all the sights."

At last I said: "I am grateful for everything you offer me. But please, do not send for the jewels, not yet. These things mean so little to me – they mean nothing, compared to what really matters."

A Proposal

"What's that?" he asked, smiling at my strangeness.

"That I can trust you, and talk to you, and that you will always be kind, and always honest with me."

For a moment, I thought a troubled look passed across his face. Then he said: "Of course. Ask me anything, Jane. What would make you happy?"

"Well," I said, "I want you to tell Mrs. Fairfax what is going on."

"My beloved, if it pleases you, I will go and talk to her now, while you prepare for our shopping trip."

I went upstairs to fetch my things, and when I came down, I saw Mr. Rochester coming out of Mrs. Fairfax's little office. I went in to see her.

She was sitting in her chair, and when she saw me she tried to smile, but soon looked worried again. I sat down opposite her. After looking at me for a while, she finally said: "Well, I am so astonished, I think perhaps I've been dreaming. Has Mr. Rochester really asked you to be his wife?"

"Yes," I said, "and I have accepted."

"Really," she said, "is this a good idea? You are not of the same class, and you are certainly not the same age. Mr. Rochester is old enough to be your father."

"He is nothing like a father to me," I objected. "He is more youthful than many a man of twenty-five!"

"And he is really marrying you for love, is he?"

This hurt me so much, my eyes filled with tears.

"I'm sorry to upset you, dear, but I must warn you to be careful. Things are not always what they seem."

At that moment, Adele ran in, begging to be allowed to come to Millcote with us. I persuaded

Mr. Rochester to let her, and the three of us set off together.

I found shopping hard work. I was not used to spending hours choosing from bright silks and satins, ribbons, trims and bonnets, and it embarrassed me. In the end I chose only two new dresses, instead of the six Mr. Rochester wanted me to have, and even then, I was glad to climb back into the carriage.

As I sat there, hot and tired, I suddenly recalled my uncle's letter. The incredible events of the last day had banished it from my mind. I must write to him as soon as I could. He was a relative, and should be told of my marriage. Furthermore, the thought of perhaps inheriting some money one day made me feel better about being showered with gifts by Mr. Rochester. If I was an independent woman, with my own wealth, I would feel more his equal.

As soon as we were back home, I sent a long letter to my uncle, explaining everything. Then I went to Mr. Rochester, and told him that I wanted to go on teaching Adele and earning my living. I was not born to be a lady of leisure. I was not a doll, to be dressed up and cosseted and draped with trinkets. I was not Celine Varens. I was Jane Eyre, a plain, hardworking governess, and I would not change.

Indeed, I resolved to be as true to myself as I possibly could in the month before the wedding, so that Mr. Rochester would have no illusions about who he was marrying. Then, if he wanted to change his mind, he could.

But the month passed by, and Mr. Rochester did not change his mind. And so it was that I found myself sitting in my room the night before my wedding day, all packed and ready for my honeymoon. Mr. Rochester had given me little cards to attach to my cases, with "Mrs. Rochester" written on them, and the name of a hotel in London – but I could not bring myself to tie them on until tomorrow. Mrs. Rochester did not yet exist.

Hanging up in my open closet was my wedding dress – a pearl-white gown. Beside it was a gossamer-fine veil, beautifully embroidered and beaded in intricate patterns. But looking at it didn't make me happy. It made me feel afraid and upset, because of something that was troubling me – something that had happened the night before.

Mr. Rochester had been away on business for the night, and that evening my dress had arrived from the dressmaker's. Sophie came running to fetch me, and all the servants gathered to see me open the box.

Underneath the dress itself, I found the beautiful veil – a surprise from Mr. Rochester. I knew he had ordered it because I had said no to the jewels. He still wanted me to have something special and expensive to wear on my wedding day.

I hung the outfit in my closet, and went to dinner. As the evening wore on, it grew dark, rainy and windy, not like summer at all. I went to bed, and as the storm battered my window, I fell into a strange and frightening dream. I dreamed that I came to Thornfield on my own, and found it was a ruin, a hollow, empty shell. I wandered through the rooms, all overgrown with weeds. Nothing of their beauty remained but old fragments of marble and plaster.

I woke up with a start; light dazzled my eyes. Someone had left a lighted candle standing on my dresser. It must be Sophie or Leah; but why?

Then I heard a noise from the closet, and saw a tall female figure walk out of it. She picked up the candle, and stood staring at my wedding gown.

My blood ran cold with horror as I realized it was not Sophie, or Leah, or Mrs. Fairfax. It was not even Grace Poole, nor anyone else I knew. This woman was tall and strong, and wore a ragged white nightdress, like a shroud. Long, dark, matted hair hung down her back.

I saw her put the candle down, then she reached up, took down the veil, and put it on her own head. Then she turned to the mirror, and that was when I saw, reflected back at me, her face — a terrifying face such as I had never seen before. I shrank back against my pillow as I stared at her insane, rolling eyes, scowling features, and purplish lips, twisted into a dreadful grimace. Then, as I watched, she took the veil off, lifted it up, and tore it into two pieces.

Lastly, taking up the candle again, she turned and headed for the door, which brought her right past my bed. She stopped, leaned over me, and looked at me

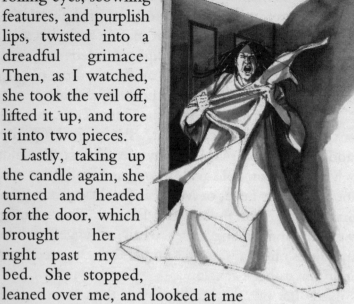

closely, her ghastly face close to mine. I was so overcome with fright that, for only the second time in my life, I fell unconscious from fear.

When I awoke, daylight had come, and my door was firmly closed. When I remembered what I had seen in the night, I was sure it had been another dream. But when I looked on the floor, I saw the veil there. It had been ripped in half.

What I had seen seemed so strange and bizarre that I was afraid to tell Mrs. Fairfax or Leah about it. I longed for Mr. Rochester to come home. I waited all day for him to return, as the wind blew stronger and the rain hammered on the roof.

When at last he came back, I opened my heart to him, and told him everything I had seen. He listened carefully, asking questions about the creature's appearance and behaviour.

Finally he said: "Jane, this is to be expected. You are anxious about your wedding, and having bad dreams. This was just another of them."

"No," I insisted. "The veil was really torn."

"Then," he answered gravely, "I am afraid the only explanation can be that it really was Grace Poole, but in your half-asleep state, you saw her differently, and imagined she was a demon."

He hugged me tightly. "What a blessing she only tore the veil," he said, "and did not harm you, my love. Yes, you are still wondering why I keep her here, and one day I will tell you – but not now. Tomorrow is our wedding day, and we must think of that."

I could not believe his words were true. I had seen the woman so vividly, so closely, and she was nothing like Grace Poole. But there was no better explanation, so I told him he must be right.

He said I should sleep in the nursery that night, with Adele and Sophie. Sophie could help me get up and dressed early in the morning.

"And no more bad dreams, Jane – you must only have happy dreams, of our future together."

So I climbed into Adele's bed, lay down next to her, and watched her in her deep, innocent slumber. True enough, that night I had no bad dreams. I had no dreams at all. I could not sleep for a moment.

The Wedding Day

In the morning, Sophie helped me to dress for my wedding. She took so long that I was nearly late, but she made me look in the mirror before I set out. The person I saw standing there, all robed in white, seemed like a stranger.

I heard Mr. Rochester calling me, and as I went down the stairs, I saw the servants taking all our cases outside to load them into the carriage.

"Are you ready?" my groom said, taking me by the hand, and leading me across the hall. Mrs. Fairfax was standing there, but I had no time to speak to her as we passed. Mr. Rochester seemed to be in a great hurry, and very determined, as if he could not relax until we were married.

It was to be a simple wedding. There were no relatives or bridesmaids – just us two, the vicar, and a clerk and his wife as witnesses. The church was close to Thornfield, but by the time Mr. Rochester had marched me there I was almost out of breath.

As we entered the churchyard, I noticed two figures wandering among the gravestones. They disappeared around the back of the church before Mr. Rochester could see them.

The Wedding Day

We walked into the dark, cool stone building and up to the little altar, where the vicar, Mr. Wood, waited for us, the witnesses beside him. Without further ado, the service began. The vicar announced that we were here to be married, then asked us if we knew of any reason why we should not be.

There was a pause, as there always is at that part of the ceremony. When is that pause ever broken? So, after a while, Mr. Wood reached out a hand to Mr. Rochester, opened his mouth and took a breath to continue with the declarations.

At that moment, a voice at the back of the church said: "The marriage cannot take place – I declare an impediment."

For a moment Mr. Rochester swayed, as if he had been struck by a blow. Then he steadied himself, looked at the vicar, and said firmly: "Proceed."

"I cannot proceed," said the vicar, "until we find out what the impediment is, and if it can be proved."

"Oh, I can prove it," said the voice.

"What is the nature of the problem?" said the vicar impatiently, peering at the shadows. "Let us sort it out at once and get on with the wedding."

"That won't be possible," said the speaker, who now stepped forward. He was a middle-aged man with a small white moustache.

"Mr. Rochester is already married," he said.

His words sliced through me like a knife blade. I managed to stay still and calm, but I felt as if my blood had frozen solid. I looked up at Mr. Rochester, and saw that same look of fixed determination on his face. Then he took my hand and pulled me closer to his side.

"Who are you?" he asked the stranger.

"I am Mr. Briggs, a solicitor from London."

"And you say I have a wife, do you?"

By way of an answer, Mr. Briggs took a folded piece of paper from his pocket, and read aloud from it the details of the marriage of Mr. Edward Fairfax Rochester to Miss Bertha Antoinetta Mason, fifteen years previously, in Jamaica.

"So I was married," Mr. Rochester snarled. "That does not mean my wife is still alive."

"She was still living three months ago," said the solicitor. "I have a witness who saw her."

Now the second figure came out of the shadows at the back of the church. It was Mr. Mason.

Mr. Rochester was still holding my hand, and I felt a wave of fury ripple through him. He stepped forward as if to strike Mason.

"Remember where you are," said the vicar sternly. Then he asked Mason: "Does he really have a wife?"

"He does," said Mason. "She lives at Thornfield Hall, and I saw her there in April. I am her brother."

"What nonsense," said the vicar angrily. "I have lived in this area for many years, and I have never heard of any Mrs. Rochester at Thornfield Hall."

Mr. Rochester was staring hard at the ground. After a long silence, he said: "You have never heard of her, because I kept her hidden. It is all true. I admit I was planning to marry again, because I wanted happiness for myself – and now my plan has been thwarted."

He looked up at them, but he could hardly bear to look at me. Then he began to speak again.

"I know that I have done a terrible thing. Wood, take off your surplice. There will be no wedding today. For I do have a wife already – if you can call her that. A wife my father forced me to marry fifteen years ago. A wife who – although they concealed it from me – is a madwoman, a wild, drunken monster.

"If you don't believe me, you can come and see her. Come on," he said, "we're going up to the house to visit her now, and you can see for yourselves why I wanted to be with this lovely girl, to be adored and treated kindly, and married to someone I would be proud to call a wife. Come on!"

Still dragging me by the hand, he strode hurriedly out of the church, with the vicar, Mr. Briggs and Mr. Mason following close behind. Outside Thornfield, Mrs. Fairfax, Leah, Sophie and Adele were waiting to greet us, but he brushed them aside impatiently. Into the house we went, up the stairs and along the hall, up the attic staircase, along the dark passageway, and finally into the room where I had nursed Mr. Mason's wounded arm. Mr. Rochester drew aside the tapestry to reveal the hidden door, opened it, and summoned us inside.

A fire burned in the grate, and over it leaned the familiar shape of Grace Poole, stirring something in a saucepan.

Beyond her, a strange creature moved to and fro, crouching and crawling on all fours. It wore a long white gown, and a tangle of matted hair hid its face.

"Hello, Mrs. Poole!" cried Mr. Rochester in a loud, cheery voice, although he was still gripping my hand, and I could feel that he was shaking. "And how is the patient today?"

"A little snappish, sir," said Grace, "but not too bad."

At this, the creature in the corner drew itself up to its full height, and began to groan and gurgle.

"She sees you," said Grace Poole. "Take care, sir."

Now the creature pulled the hair away from its face, and I knew for certain it was the strange woman who had come into my room the night

before last. She bellowed that now familiar loud, monstrous laugh, then suddenly leaped forward, seized Mr. Rochester around the neck and tried to throttle him, shrieking in a high-pitched wail. He could have beaten her off, but he would not strike her; instead he wrestled her into a chair, and Grace Poole quickly tied her down.

Mr. Rochester turned to us, his face hot and red.

"Meet my wife, Bertha," he said. "This is her. This is all I have for a life's companion — and these roars and attacks are all the endearments I can expect. And this," he added, coming over to me, "this is what I wanted — this sweet, kind young lady to be my own. Look at her, and blame me if you can. Now, leave me, while I sort out matters here."

In silence, the vicar, the two gentlemen and I left the room and descended the attic stairs. In the lower hallway, Mr. Briggs said: "You are not to blame for any of this, Miss Eyre. I can see you knew nothing of the marriage. And your uncle will be glad to hear it."

"My uncle?" I was confused. "But – how do you know about him?"

"Your uncle is a friend of Mr. Mason. When he received your letter, he told Mr. Mason about the wedding. They realized what was going on, and Mason came to intervene. We arrived just in time."

"My uncle did not write to me," I said faintly.

"I am sure he will," said Mr. Briggs. "But he himself is very sick, and may not recover. You must wait for news about his state of health."

Then they all took their leave, and I found myself standing in the hallway, alone. I went into my room and bolted the door.

I was in too much shock to cry. Instead, I calmly took off my white gown, and put on the plain dress I had been wearing the day before. Then I sat down, laid my head on my arms and thought hard about what had happened.

I knew I was the same person I had been an hour ago; but my future was gone. My life was changed forever. There was still love for Mr. Rochester in my heart, but it was like a sick child, or a cold, trembling animal that could not be revived. I could no longer trust him, and I must go away from him – that much

I was sure of. How, where, what I would do I did not know, but I could not stay here. I was, as I had always really been, alone, and I must fend for myself now. There was no one to help me.

At last, my sorrow swept over me in a huge wave, and I wept and sobbed for my lost love, my destroyed dreams, and my poor, ruined hopes.

I stayed locked away in my room until the afternoon, when I began to wonder why no one had knocked at my door, or come to comfort me. I wiped my face, unbolted my door, and opened it.

Mr. Rochester was sitting outside, on a chair he had placed in the hallway. He jumped up.

"Jane – I have been waiting for you all this time," he said. "Why did you not scream and shout at me?"

I said nothing. I couldn't speak.

"I never meant to hurt you, Jane; I love you. I hoped I could have happiness with you – I was a fool. I am so sorry, Jane. Can you forgive me?"

I looked up into his eyes. They were so full of sadness and remorse, I couldn't help but forgive him at once. But I did not tell him so.

"I would like a drink of water," I said.

He took me to the library to sit down, and brought me something to eat and drink. It made me feel stronger, but when I looked at him I was overcome with grief. I knew I had to go, but I loved him so much.

He tried to kiss me, but I turned away.

"Don't you still love me, Jane?"

"Of course I do," I whispered, tears filling my eyes. "But I cannot stay here now."

"I understand," he said. "Nor can I. I will leave Grace Poole in charge of Thornfield, and go. I have another house, called Fearndean, to live in."

"Then take Adele with you when you go," I said, sobbing. "You'll need the company."

"But you will come with me, Jane, won't you? We'll live there together."

"No, I will not. I love you, but I cannot live with you while you have a wife. I will not be a mistress."

"We will be just like a real husband and wife. We belong together far more than she and I ever did. Please, Jane!" he cried, kneeling on the library floor.

"No."

Over and over he begged me to stay with him, to comfort him, to be with him forever – and I longed to say yes. But I could not. My trust in him had been ruined. Nothing was what I had thought it was. I stood up and walked to the door.

"Farewell," I said quietly, and went to my room.

I was awake long before anyone else. I put on a simple dress, a straw bonnet and a shawl, and taking my purse and a small bag of possessions, I crept downstairs. I whispered a last goodbye to Adele and Mrs. Fairfax as I passed their rooms, and left the house. I ran across the fields, heading for the road that lead in the opposite direction from Millcote. I had never been that way before.

I thought of Mr. Rochester waking up in his

room, and I longed to go to him and say yes after all. But I knew I must not. Although it broke my heart, I went on running.

I came to the road, and saw a coach coming. I stopped it and asked the driver to carry me as far as I could go for 20 shillings – all the money I had in my purse. I climbed in, and wept bitterly as the coach carried me away from the man I loved, and the life I had longed for.

The Runaway

The coach drove all day, until at last the distance I had paid for was used up. The driver let me out at a place called Whitecross. It was not a town, nor even a village or a hamlet. It was just a set of crossroads, with a white-painted signpost pointing in four directions. The nearest town it named was ten miles away, and the others were even further off.

All around me was moor and heathland, with mountains in the distance. There was not a soul to be seen, and I knew I did not have time to walk ten miles before nightfall. I was alone with nature – so, for tonight, nature would have to be my host.

I set out across the moor, following the line of a stream, until I came to a craggy rock leaning out of the ground at an angle, and sat down beneath it. The heather and the mossy grass were dry, and still warm from the heat of the afternoon.

I had eaten nothing all day except a hunk of bread I had taken from the kitchen, and it was nearly gone. But there were bilberry bushes close by, and I gathered two handfuls of berries to eat with my crust, and drank water from the stream.

Then I lay down next to the rock, on the springy

heather, with a grassy tussock for a pillow, and spread my shawl over me, folded in two. In this makeshift bed I was comfortable enough to sleep – or I would have been, if it were not for my broken heart.

As I closed my eyes, I could not keep thoughts of Mr. Rochester from flowing into my mind. I saw his face before me, begging and pleading, and I shook with grief, longing and disappointment. How could everything be so different now, from the way it had appeared just a few days ago?

I wept for a while, then opened my eyes and stared up into the dark sky. I saw the Milky Way, vast and silent, and remembered that I was not really alone. I said a prayer, asking God to help me in my troubles, and to comfort Mr. Rochester in his. Finally, I curled up in my nest of moss and heather, and fell into a deep sleep.

Long after the sun had risen, and the birds had started to sing, I stirred, awoke, and remembered where I was. It was a still, hot, perfect morning. I heard a bee buzzing among the bilberry bushes, and saw a little brown lizard sitting on the rock next to me. I wished I could be one of them, so that this moor could give me everything I needed to survive, and I could stay here forever. Then, for a moment, I wished that God had seen fit to take my soul in the night, so that this could have been my resting-place, and I would have to suffer no longer.

But I was alive, and I had to find myself work of some kind. So I stood up, put on my shawl and bonnet, and tramped back to the road. I did not look at the signpost again. Instead, I simply chose the road that led away from the sun, so that it would not shine into my eyes, and walked and walked.

After several miles, I had seen no houses or people, and the sun was high overhead, so I sat down on a stone to rest. Just as I was thinking I was too hot and tired to go on, and would have to find a place to sleep nearby, I heard a church bell.

I turned and saw a pale spire among the moorland hills, where I had noticed nothing before. I set off over the moors towards it, and soon came across a little village.

As I walked down the main street, I knew I looked like a respectable lady, with my nice dress, bonnet and shawl. But hunger gnawed away at my insides, and I had not a penny to my name. In truth, I was no more than a poor vagrant. If I wanted food, I would have to beg for it.

Or, I thought suddenly, perhaps I could exchange one of my few possessions for something to eat. I had a silk handkerchief, and a pair of good leather gloves, though they were hardly valuable.

I stopped outside a baker's shop, with a row of bread cakes in the window. I wanted one of them so desperately that I pushed open the door and went in. The smell of new–baked bread made me want to cry.

"Good afternoon, Miss," said the woman behind the counter cheerily. She, of course, saw me as a customer with money to spend, and all of a sudden I felt ridiculous. I could not possibly offer her my used handkerchief, my worn gloves, in place of payment.

"I – I was feeling hot, and wondered if I might sit down in here for a moment," I stammered.

"I suppose so," said the woman, sounding slightly put out, and I sat down in a chair near the door. After a while, I plucked up the courage to ask: "Do you know, by any chance, if anyone in this village is looking for domestic help, or a governess?"

"I couldn't say, Miss."

"Is there any other work in the village?"

"There's Oliver's needle factory, and farmhanding. But that's men's work," she added, with a distrustful look.

Soon another woman came in and started chatting to the shopkeeper. I felt like a nuisance, so I left.

I wandered around the village. At the end of the main street I saw a large, pretty house, and asked if they needed a servant. "We don't have no servants," said the young woman who came to the door. I came back past the church again, and when I saw the vicarage, I thought of asking the vicar for advice. Surely, I reasoned, that was part of a vicar's job – to help those who were lost and in need? But when I knocked, there was no answer.

I set off again, feeling more and more desperate and tearful. When would someone be kind and friendly to me? As the evening wore on, and the shops began to close, I headed out of the village and up a lane leading to the moors, thinking I would have to sleep there again.

After a while, I came past a little farmhouse, and

saw a man sitting outside the door, having his supper. Next to him on a little table were half a loaf of bread and a block of cheese.

By now, I was so hungry I could not stop myself. I leaned over the wall and called: "Please will you give me a piece of your bread, sir? I'm very hungry."

The man looked surprised for a moment, but he took up his knife, cut a thick slice of bread, and a little cheese to go with it, and brought it over to me. I don't believe he thought I was a beggar at all. He probably thought I was just an eccentric lady out for a walk, who suddenly felt like a snack. So, hoping to retain my dignity, I thanked him kindly, and walked on at a measured pace. But, as soon as I was out of sight, I devoured that bread and cheese as if I were a starved animal.

As I finished it, I felt the first few drops of a summer rainstorm. The sky was dark, and now that the sun was going down, I began to feel cold. In bad weather, it would not be nearly so easy to spend a night out of doors. I had no idea what to do.

I walked on and on, up the lane and back into moorland country. Darkness fell, and the rain grew heavier. I had no way of keeping dry, and I knew that if I stayed out in the storm, I was in danger of catching a cold, but I had no choice. I pressed on, looking for some kind of bush or rock to shelter me.

Then I saw a glowing light ahead. At first I thought my mind was playing tricks on me; or that it was one of the ghostly lights that appear on the moors when marsh gases catch fire. But it stayed steady, so I made my way toward it.

It was pitch-dark by now, and I could barely see my way. I splashed across a bog, and twice I fell down in the mud. I felt my way up a steep slope, past bushes and rocks, until at last, I saw that the light came from a little window, and against the black sky I could just make out the even blacker shape of a long, low cottage. Reaching out my hands, I found a rough garden wall, and moved along it until I came to the gate. I went up to the window, and looked in.

Inside I saw a little kitchen, clean and bright, with a sanded floor and a polished dresser. In front of the window was a table with a candle on it. An old woman sat there, knitting a stocking, and beyond her I saw a fireplace with a bright fire burning.

Sitting beside it were two younger ladies, both dressed in black, with a dog at their feet.

I saw them talking and heard their voices, though I could not hear what they said. Then the older woman got up and started to prepare supper. That reminded me of my own reduced state, and I realized that if I was going to ask them for help, I had better do it now, before they all went to bed.

I knocked at the door. The old woman answered.

"May I speak to the two young ladies?" I asked.

"You can speak to me. What do you want?"

"Please, ma'am, I need shelter, and a morsel to eat."

"I'll give you a penny," she said, taking one from her pocket and handing it over, "but you can't stay here." She looked me up and down suspiciously. "And if you've some fellows with you, hiding in the bushes, who are planning to rob us, you can tell them not to bother. The master of the house will be back soon, and we've a dog, you know, and a gun."

Then she slammed and bolted the door.

"No!" I cried, falling to my knees on the wet paving stones. "Please! I will die if I stay out here!"

"We will all die anyhow, in the end," said a voice behind me. "But to die so soon would be a shame."

I turned and saw, through the dark and rain, a tall man coming up the path. He helped me to my feet, knocked on the door and called: "It is I! St. John!"

The old woman opened the door again.

"Hannah, thank you for guarding us against attack, but I believe this young lady is in true need," he told her, and led me into the house.

Soon I was sitting before that warm hearth myself, surrounded by all four strangers. I knew I must look shocking to them. I was weak and exhausted, my face was tearstained, and my dress was soaked and smeared with mud. But although they all looked amazed, they were not unkind. One of the two young ladies made me some hot milk and toast.

"I am Diana Rivers," she said. "This is my brother St. John, and my sister Mary. What is your name?"

"It is Jane," I said. "Jane Elliot."

"Are you lost? Can we send for your family or friends?" asked St. John.

"There is no one."

"How did you come here?" asked Mary, taking my hand gently. But I could speak no more. I began to tremble and feel faint, and at St. John's direction, Hannah took my plate and helped me up the stairs. Before I knew what was happening, I was sound asleep in a safe, warm, dry bed.

A New Life

I had caught a fever, and I spent the next three days and nights in bed, barely conscious. The two sisters often came in to sit at my bedside, and sometimes I would hear them talking about me.

"Poor little thing," said one of them. "I wonder what happened to her, and how she ended up here?"

"She would have died if she hadn't found us."

"I like her face – you know, if she weren't so exhausted and ill, she'd have quite a bold look."

They didn't know I could hear them, but never did they once speak a word of disapproval, or say they regretted taking me in.

On the fourth day, I was well enough to eat some porridge and, the day after that, I woke up in the morning feeling much better. My dress was hanging on the back of a chair, freshly washed. When I put it on, it was too big for me, as I had eaten hardly anything for a week. But I found a comb and smoothed my hair, and went downstairs.

The house was filled with the smell of baking, and I found Hannah in the kitchen, hard at work. Although our first meeting had not gone well, she smiled at me now. After she had sat me down by the fire, she started asking me questions.

"Had you been a-begging before you came here?"

"I'm not a beggar – not really."

"Are you book-learned, then?" she asked.

"Yes, I was at boarding school for eight years."

"Really! Then why do you not keep yourself?"

"I have done, and I will again," I said. "I mean to support myself as soon as I can."

"Well then," she said, "I'm right sorry I doubted you. It's just there's so many rogues and cheats about, I took you for a vagabond."

She gave me her floury hand to shake, and from that moment on we were friends.

Then she told me that old Mr. Rivers, the father of Diana, Mary and St. John, had recently died, which explained their mourning clothes. Their mother had died many years ago, and Hannah had been their nurse since they were little. St. John was to take his father's place as vicar of Morton, the nearby village, and would soon move into the very vicarage I had called at. Diana and Mary were both governesses, and were usually away, but had come home for their father's funeral.

At that moment St. John and his sisters came in from walking. They made a great fuss of me and said that, as a guest, I must not sit in the kitchen. Diana took me into the drawing room, and left me there with St. John while she went to make some tea.

St. John was reading, and I was able to study him closely. He was about twenty-eight, tall and slim, with a face like a Greek statue. He had pale eyes, a long, straight nose, and a broad forehead surrounded by fair curls. But although he was handsome, there was something cold and hard about him.

Diana came in with tea and cakes, and Mary soon joined us. Before we ate, I thanked them all heartily for their kindness, and said I hoped I would not have to impose on them for too much longer.

"As soon as you are ready," said St. John, "you can tell us where you live, and we'll take you home."

"I'm afraid I cannot," I said, "for I have no home."

"None at all?" he asked. "Are you a spinster?"

"Why, St. John, she's hardly old enough to be married!" Diana said, laughing at his seriousness.

"I'm not married," I said, but the thought of this made tears come to my eyes.

"Don't question poor Miss Elliot so," said Mary.

"I will tell you more," I said, quietly. "I was at Lowood School, and worked there as a teacher. Then I went to be a governess, and I found a good position. But, four days ago, I had to leave. I cannot tell you why. I did no wrong – I am not a criminal. But it is not possible for me to look to the past. I must find work, and make my own living again."

Now St. John was looking at me with a new interest. "You're a governess?" he asked. "A teacher?"

"Oh, St. John!" said Diana excitedly. "Do you think she might work at the new school?"

"Miss Elliot," St. John continued, "when my father came to Morton, some years ago, it had no school, but he managed to establish one – a church school, for the boys of the town. It is paid for by Miss

Oliver, whose father owns a needle factory."

"Oliver's needle factory!" I said. "I've heard of it."

He looked surprised, but went on: "Following my father's death, Miss Oliver has offered to provide the funds for a second school – a school for girls. It is to be opened in a month's time, and I have not yet found a teacher for it. The pay will be thirty pounds a year, and there is a cottage for the schoolmistress to live in. Could you be this schoolmistress?"

"Oh, Mr. Rivers," I cried, my heart filling with relief. "I must thank you from the bottom of my heart for this offer. And I accept!"

And so I spent a month longer living at Moor House with my new friends, before we were to go our separate ways – Diana and Mary back to their employers, St. John and Hannah to the vicarage, and I to my cottage and my new job.

And the more I knew them, the more I liked them. I shared so much with Diana and Mary, it was as if I had known them all my life. We all loved to read, and we often went walking on the moors, and they admired my painting and drawing. We found it easy to sit and talk for hours together every evening.

St. John, though, was not at home so much. He spent most of his time visiting his new parishioners, who were scattered across the countryside. When he was in, he often seemed gloomy and serious. While his sisters delighted in the wild birds and flowers of the moor, and loved to see me paint them, he barely took an interest in the wonders of nature. His mind always seemed to be working on a higher level; his large, cold eyes concentrated on other thoughts.

The weeks passed by quickly, and Diana and Mary grew sad at the thought of having to leave. They told me that this parting from St. John would be harder than any they had undergone before.

"You see, it will not be very long before he goes abroad," Diana explained. "He plans to be a missionary, in India. And, once he has gone, who knows when we will see him again?"

Just then, St. John came in, looking even more serious than usual. He had a letter in his hand.

"What is it, brother?" Diana asked.

"Uncle John is dead," he said, bluntly.

Diana and Mary looked taken aback, although not at all upset. "And...?" asked Mary.

"And nothing," said St. John firmly. "He has left his whole fortune to another relation."

Then Diana said to me, "Jane, you will think us heartless not to mourn our uncle. But you see, we never knew him. He was our mother's brother, and after she died, he argued with our father and went abroad. Our father hoped that our uncle would eventually leave us some of his money. And if he had, we would all be able to relax a little, for we are far from wealthy. So you see, we are disappointed."

"Well, he leaves us nothing," said St. John again. "And that is that."

A few weeks later, I was settled into my new life as Miss Elliot, village schoolmistress at Morton. My students were simple village girls and farmer's daughters, and when they came to me, hardly any of them could read a word – but they tried hard. They loved to knit and sew and sing, and my little school buzzed with activity from morning to night. Rosamund Oliver, the school's patron, often visited us, and St. John came every day to teach an hour of scripture. The villagers always greeted me politely in the street and doffed their caps to me. I had money to live on, and I was warm, safe and happy – or at least, as happy as I thought I would ever be.

Of course, not a moment went by when I did not think of Mr. Rochester. I dreamed about him by day and by night, and his face never faded from my mind. How I missed him! I often wondered what my life might be like if I had chosen differently, and gone to live with him as his mistress. But a part of me always knew that I had made the right choice.

And so the months passed by, and summer turned

to autumn, and autumn to winter. November the fifth was a holiday and, after doing some cleaning and baking, I sat down at my table to finish a miniature of Miss Oliver. I had drawn her from life a week previously, and now I was adding paint to the sketch, which I planned to give her as a present.

I was filling in the dark blue of her silk dress when there was a quick tap at the door. Before I could get up to answer it, St. John Rivers stepped in.

"I have come to see how you are spending your holiday," he said. "At your painting, as I expected."

"It is a picture of Rosamund Oliver," I said, turning it to show him, "but I'm afraid I haven't quite captured her. Don't you think she's beautiful?"

"Hmmm," St. John mumbled. I suspected that he and Miss Oliver liked each other, and wondered if they would get married. I did not dare drop any more hints, but St. John had guessed at my meaning.

"Miss Elliot," he said, and I looked up. "You know, or at least I imagine my sisters have told you, that I plan to travel to India to be a missionary. If I marry at all, it must be to someone who is used to hardship. I'm afraid Miss Oliver would not do, lovely as she is. But enough of that. I'm here for another reason."

"What is that?"

"To see your artworks. I have been meaning for some time to ask you if I could look at them."

I was surprised. He had never shown the slightest interest in my pictures before. But I got up and fetched a folder full of drawings, and gave it to him.

St. John remained standing as he leafed through them. "Very good," he murmured.

I was again absorbed in my work when I heard a little tearing sound, and looked up. St. John, holding up a small sketch, had torn off a corner of the paper. He seemed alive with excitement. It was quite unlike any expression I had seen on his face before.

"I knew you would sign your work, like any good artist," he said. "But it is not signed 'Jane Elliot', is it?"

I blushed deeply, and felt my heart thumping.

"St. John, I'm so sorry to have deceived you," I said. "You see I – I simply didn't want someone... I mean anyone, to find me here. I can explain."

"No need, Miss Eyre, I am sure you had your reasons. It is not your falsehood I am interested in, but the truth. You are Miss Jane Eyre, formerly of Gateshead Hall, and Thornfield Hall?"

"How do you know?!" I gasped.

"It is all in my late uncle's will," he said. "My uncle John Eyre, of Madeira."

"What?" I felt unsteady; the room seemed to spin.

"Our uncle on our mother's side, and yours on your father's side," he said. "And you, Jane, are the poor orphan to whom he left his fortune. All of it."

"How did you guess?" I asked, my voice a whisper.

"I thought I glimpsed the name on your drawings, and I decided to come and find out for certain."

"And you, Diana, and Mary – you are my cousins?"

"It would seem so," St. John said, allowing himself a smile. "But you have more than cousins, Jane. You have twenty thousand pounds. You are a rich lady."

A Rich Lady

Twenty thousand pounds! It was more money than I could possibly imagine. And yet more important to me than that, much more, was the fact that I had a real family, that my dear Diana and Mary and St. John were my own blood relatives.

And now, I realized, I could truly thank them for saving my life, and for the unending kindness and hospitality they had shown me. What did I want with twenty thousand pounds? It was far more than anybody needed. I resolved to split the inheritance between us all, so that John Eyre's four relatives would have five thousand pounds each. It would be enough to keep us for the rest of our lives.

I told St. John of my plan at once, and asked him to write to Diana and Mary to tell them that, if they wished, they could stop working and come home. At first he protested, saying that our uncle had left the money to me, and so it was mine.

"Don't you realize what twenty thousand pounds could do for you?" he asked. "You could buy a fine house, and become a lady of standing in society."

"But I don't want to be a lady of standing in society," I said. "I would rather live at Moor House

158

with my cousins, and stay the way I am."

"Will you still be the schoolmistress?"

I reflected. I knew I wanted to study, and travel one day, and have time for myself. So I said: "I will stay at the school until Christmas, to give you time to find another teacher."

And so a lawyer was sent for; he wrote to uncle Eyre's solicitors and, within a few weeks, St. John, Diana, Mary and I had five thousand pounds each to our names.

In early December, I shut up the school. Another teacher had been found to start in the new year, and I said farewell to my students. I eased my conscience by giving the school a gift of money, left my cottage tidy, and returned to Moor House.

My plan was to clean the house from top to bottom, and prepare it beautifully for Diana and Mary's return. They had given up their posts, and were to arrive home a week before Christmas. I spent a little of my unexpected wealth on new carpets and furniture. Then I put on an apron and scrubbed and polished every inch of the house until it sparkled. With two days to spare, I sent for Hannah from the vicarage, and we spent every moment baking Christmas cakes, pies and puddings, building fires in every grate, hanging up decorations and setting out candles.

When at last the evening of their arrival came, Hannah, St. John and I waited outside to greet their carriage. How happy I was when it finally drew up outside the door and Many and Diana climbed out, exclaiming over the decorations and lights that filled the house, kissing me and their brother and welcoming me as their long–lost cousin. It was the happiest Christmas I had ever known. As the snow fell and the wind roared outside, our little home overflowed with talking and laughter.

St. John, of course, did not join in with the celebrations quite so cheerfully as his sisters. No amount of money would dissuade him from his ambition to be a missionary, and his mind was mostly occupied with his plans. He meant to set off some time in the coming year.

Through the spring, Mary, Diana and I lived at Moor House, while St. John and Hannah returned to the vicarage, although they visited us often. I did not plan to spend my whole life as a lady of leisure, but what a relief it was, just for those few months, to spend my time as I pleased. I drew, and painted, and walked on the moors, and enjoyed my cousins' company every day. And, helped by Diana, I began to learn German, which I was sure would be useful when I was ready to see a little more of the world.

One evening, as Diana, Mary and I studied in the drawing room, St. John came in and asked me how my knowledge of German was proceeding.

"She is doing very well," said Diana. "She has a natural aptitude for languages."

"Well then, Jane," St. John declared, "I would like you to stop learning German, and start learning Hindustani."

"Hindustani? Me?" I said. "Why?"

"What can you mean by it, brother?" asked Mary.

"My plans are settled," he replied, "and I will leave for India soon. I am learning Hindustani myself, but I need some help with it. I need a study partner. I have considered asking each of you, but I think Jane is best suited to the task."

Diana laughed out loud. "Well, it's just as well you didn't ask me," she said. "I wouldn't be persuaded to learn Hindustani for a moment – it's far too hard!"

"Of course it is," said Mary. "Don't let him bully you into such a thing, Jane!"

But something about St. John's cold eyes, and the stern way he spoke, made me feel I had to obey him. I didn't know how to refuse.

And so we began studying Hindustani together. Several times a week, when he was not busy with his parish work, he would come up to Moor House with his books, and oblige me to join him for a lesson. I was good at languages, and I had enjoyed German, but now I felt challenged beyond my abilities. Yet St. John was so strict and demanding, I struggled to please him, and didn't dare to say no.

And did spending so much time with St. John Rivers make me forget Mr. Rochester? Oh no – the opposite was true.

Since my fortunes had changed, and I had grown more settled, I thought of him more and more. Although I knew I must not visit him, I longed to know if he was well, if he was happy. And so I had decided to write to Mrs. Fairfax, in confidence, to ask how things were at Thornfield.

A month had passed with no answer. This alarmed me, as I knew Mrs. Fairfax loved writing letters. I had been sure she would reply at once.

I thought perhaps she hadn't received my letter, so I wrote again. Again, I heard nothing. As the weeks went by, I became more and more anxious. My fears gnawed at my heart even as I sat with St. John, day after day, and battled with my Hindustani verbs.

Diana and Mary noticed that something was troubling me, and asked what it was, but I couldn't say. Then, one late spring morning, as St. John and I studied together, I found myself dwelling so deeply on my thoughts of Thornfield that I began to cry.

When he saw my tears, my cousin was as calm and cool as ever. "We shall put away the books, Jane, as you are clearly overtaxed," he said. "Let us take a walk upon the moor instead."

"I'll fetch Diana and Mary," I sniffed, getting up and wiping my eyes.

"No," he said. "It will be just you and me."

The sun was shining as we set out, but the heather was damp and dewy, and there was a strong breeze. I was glad I had brought my cloak.

We left the path and walked up a hillside meadow where tiny white and yellow flowers dotted the ground, until we came to a clear stream tumbling down over mossy boulders. I sat down on a rock to rest, while St. John remained standing. He slowly turned around, surveying the countryside that he would soon be leaving behind – perhaps forever.

"I set sail in six weeks, Jane," he said, over the noise of the stream.

"And I wish you good luck, cousin," I replied. "Only a few people are fit for such an adventure."

"Well," he said, with a rare smile, "I cannot afford to dwell on those who are too weak to travel to India. I am thinking only of those who are strong enough for it."

I was not sure what he meant, but I had an idea what it might be, and my heart sank.

"Surely if someone is suited to such work, their hearts will tell them so," I said.

"And what does your heart say, Jane?"

So I was right. "Nothing at all," I answered. "My heart has nothing to say on the matter."

"Then I must speak for it," he said, coming around and standing before me. "Jane, you must come with me to India, to be my companion and my assistant – to be my wife. I want you to marry me."

"No!" I responded at once, a little too hastily. I tried to explain. "I cannot, St. John; I do not want to go to India," I went on, although I felt his cold eyes on me, and found it very hard to defy him.

"But you are brave, hardworking and honest – I feel you were born to be a missionary's wife."

"No," I said again, but I could not look at him.

He had more to say, though. "Jane, it is not for my own pleasure that I ask you this – it is for the service of God. It is because you are so well suited to the position..."

This was even worse. I saw that St. John was prepared to marry me, even though he felt no passion for me, simply because he wanted help with his holy work.

I shook my head again and again, but he had more arguments ready. Had I not said I wished to travel? Now that I had money, and did not need to work, should I not use my life to do some good in the world? And were not he and I similar, in our interests, and our natures?

I did not think so at all. I closed my eyes against his reasons, and inside my head I thought of Mr. Rochester, and how he had loved me with a true heart full of feeling, so unlike St. John's cold, logical reasoning. And I still loved him back. But I could see

that, as long as I did so, I would be in danger. I would have to resist the temptation of returning, and suffer the agony of longing to hear about him.

If I were married, and gone to India, I could never be tempted to go back to him. And wasn't St. John right, that it would be a noble and useful way to spend my life? Even though I didn't love St. John – not as anything more than a cousin? Even though the thought of being married to him was –

"You *will* be my wife, Jane," I heard him say, very close to me now. My eyes were still closed, but I felt him lay a hand on top of my head, and rest it there. It felt almost as if he were hypnotizing me – as if some strange power of control flowed from his hand, and I began to feel subdued, compelled, forced to obey him...

"Jane! Jane! Jane!"

Mr. Rochester's voice rang through my head so clearly that for a second I could have sworn he was there on the moor with us. I opened my eyes and stood up at once, shaking St. John's hand away from me; and my eyes darted around and scanned the horizon. There no one was in sight.

Had the voice been inside my head? I wasn't sure, but I was certain I had heard him calling me, calling me with such longing and desperation that I suddenly knew I had to go to him, now, whatever the cost, whatever was right or wrong.

I pulled my shawl tightly around me and, ignoring St. John's shouts of protest, I ran away across the moor, down the hillside and back to the house.

Mrs. Rochester

That night, when I had calmed down, I told my cousins I had to visit a friend, and would be gone a few days. I knew they might think this strange, since I had said I didn't have any friends, but they didn't remark on it. Diana just asked: "Are you sure you are fit to travel? You look pale." I assured her that I was.

And so I rose early the next morning, and packed my bag. As I left my room, I found a note slipped under my door. It read:

> *Jane,*
>
> *I will wait to hear your final decision when you return. In the meantime, I will pray for you.*
>
> *Yours ever,*
> *St. John Rivers*

I folded the note into my pocket, left the house, and set out across the moors in the dawn light. An hour later, I had reached the signpost at Whitecross.

I realized it was almost a year since I had first arrived at that same spot, desolate and lonely, with no idea what might become of me. Who could have guessed things would turn out as they had, and that

I would now be so much happier?

And yet, as the coach drew up, and I climbed in, and the wheels began to turn to carry me in the direction of Millcote, I felt as if I was going home.

By late afternoon, I saw familiar landscapes around me. When the coach stopped at a wayside inn I knew, I climbed out, saying I would walk from there. Thornfield was less than a mile away.

I am nearly there, I thought to myself, as I set off across the fields. *I will see him soon.*

But then other thoughts crowded into my head. *What makes you think he will be there?* I scolded myself. *Mr. Rochester could be abroad — he could be away visiting friends. The voice you heard was only in your head — of course he could not really have called you. Your silly hopes are built on a dream — on nothing.*

For a moment I faltered. I was stupid to have come back, after I had fled so suddenly, and vowed never to see Mr. Rochester again. What was I doing? If I wanted to know how he was, any local person could tell me. There was no need for anyone at Thornfield to see me at all. I must turn back.

But I couldn't stop. Something was pulling me on, and I grew desperate to reach the house. I longed to see the orchard, the rookery, the thorn trees, and the high battlements. I kept walking.

As I came nearer, I came across individual stones and trees that I remembered from before, and they filled me with such emotion that I broke into a run. I hurried along behind the orchard wall, hearing the rooks cawing close by. I knew that when I turned at the end of the wall, I would see the house. I could not help but think I might see Mr. Rochester too, standing in his window, or walking on the lawn.

I reached the end of the orchard, and ran around the corner onto the path that led up to the house. Then I stumbled to a halt, and stood there helplessly on the path, gazing in horror at what I saw.

Thornfield Hall was an empty, blackened ruin.

The front of the house still rose up, high and grand, but its windows were empty of glass, and its broken stonework was dark with soot and tufted with weeds. Behind the gaping doorway lay heaps of rubble, overgrown with moss, where the roof and the chimneys had fallen down.

I began to walk forward again, no longer eager, but distraught and disbelieving. I crossed the lawn, staring up at the shell of the house. Silence surrounded me, broken only by the cries of the

rooks as they circled around the deserted building.

Thornfield had clearly been destroyed by a great fire. But now I could hardly bear the thought that came into my head: had the fire taken lives as well as property? I had to know what had happened. I turned and ran all the way back to the inn, and asked the owner if he could answer some questions I had.

"Of course, Miss – how can I help?"

"Do you know Thornfield Hall?" I asked. "I used to work there."

"Did you? Why, so did I – many years ago now," he said. "I was the late Mr. Rochester's butler."

"The late Mr. Rochester?" I gasped, feeling every bone in my body turn cold.

"Ah, you misunderstand me. I mean old Mr. Rochester, the present Mr. Rochester's father."

I breathed again. Mr. Rochester was alive after all.

"So... is the present Mr. Rochester still living at Thornfield?" I asked. Of course, I knew he could not be, but I wanted to hear the whole story.

"Oh no – no one's living there. Have you not heard about the fire?"

"I've been away for some time."

"Oh, Miss, I'm afraid the house has been burned to the ground! It was last autumn, about harvest time. A fire started in the night, and before they could bring the fire engines from Millcote it was all ablaze. I saw it myself. Such a shame – nothing could be saved. All that fine furniture, burned to a crisp!"

"How did the fire start?"

"Well, it was a shady business, Miss. I don't know

if you ever heard any gossip that Mr. Rochester kept a strange lady in secret at the house – a lunatic?"

"I... I did hear something about that."

"Yes, well it was talked of for years, though no one knew who she was. But, just a year ago, there was a scandal, for it turned out she was his wife! He'd fallen for another lady – his governess, they said – I never saw her myself, but the servants said they'd never seen him so in love. He wanted to marry her, you see, and he never told her he had a wife. Well, they got as far as the church, but then it all came out, and the wedding was called off."

"But the fire," I interrupted. "Did Mr. Rochester's wife have something to do with it?"

"You've got it in one, Miss – it was her that started it. You see, they had a servant to watch her – Grace Poole, her name was – and a good job she did too, except for one thing: she liked a drink. She'd fall asleep after she'd been drinking late at night, and the madwoman would steal the keys from her pocket, and wander through the house, causing mischief.

"Well, after all the fuss, the governess ran off, and Mr. Rochester almost went insane himself looking for her, but he couldn't find her. So he sent the little girl to school, and shut himself up in Thornfield like a hermit. And then the fire happened. Mrs. Rochester got out again, took a candle, and set light to one of the beds – I heard it was the one in the governess's room, as if she were taking her revenge. But of course the girl was long gone by then."

"So Rochester was at home when the fire started?"

"Oh yes, and they say he was as brave as a lion – he pulled all the servants from their beds and carried them outside, and then he went back in for his wife. But she had run up on the roof – we could see her dancing in the flames – and he tried to catch her to bring her back safe, but she leaped from the top, and fell down and died. It was dreadful, Miss."

"How awful," I said. "And... did anyone else die?"

"No, but it might have been as well if they had."

"What do you mean?"

"I mean Mr. Rochester, Miss – for he suffered cruelly. Well, he had to escape, but as he was coming down the staircase, it gave way, and he fell in the fire. His face was burned, and he's blind as a bat to this day. Some say it's his punishment for keeping that wife of his a secret, but I say, if it is, it's a harsh one. He tried to do his best by her, and no mistake."

"And what happened to him? Where did he go?"

"Why, he is gone to live at Fearndean, his other house, twenty miles off. And they say he lives a life of misery, now he has lost his sight, and his wife, and his lady-love too. He only has old John and Mary to care for him, for he sent all the other servants away."

"Do you have a carriage for hire?" I asked.

"Of course, Miss, it's outside."

"I know it's late," I said, "but I will pay you double if you can find someone to drive me to Fearndean now, and take me there before sunset."

Fearndean was in a forest, and after the coachman left me at the gates, I walked up a grassy track for half a mile before I saw the house. It was smaller than Thornfield, and plain and simple. It looked empty.

I knocked on the door. Dusk was falling, and it had started to rain. Then the door opened, and John's wife Mary appeared. Her mouth fell open. "Miss Eyre!" she exclaimed. "Why, is it really you?"

I explained that I had heard about the fire, and come to visit Mr. Rochester. But I asked her not to tell him who I was. I wanted to surprise him.

"You'll find him much changed, I fear," she said. But she agreed to let me carry in a jug of water that she had been about to take to him. She opened the drawing-room door for me, and I went in.

Mr. Rochester was sitting in an armchair, facing away from me. Straight away, Pilot got up from the hearth and came to me, wagging his tail.

"Down, Pilot – what is it?" My heart melted to hear his voice again, as rich and deep as ever.

He turned around – an automatic gesture, for he could not see. But I could see him. His face was scarred, his eyes half-closed. My heart leapt in my chest, and my hands shook as I put the jug down.

"That is you, isn't it, Mary?"

"Mary is in the kitchen," I said.

He jumped. "Who is that? Who is there?"

"Well, Pilot knows who I am," I said, smiling, "and Mary recognized me. I've brought your water, sir."

"It cannot be – it is a delusion," he said, stretching out his hands. I reached out and touched them.

"It is her hand!" he said, and pulled me closer. "This is her shape! Jane... is it you? Am I dreaming?"

"It is me, Edward – it is really me!"

"Jane – I thought you would never come back..."

My eyes were full of tears, and now they fell, splashing onto his hands and face. "I never will run away again," I sobbed. "I will never leave you."

And so we were reunited. He hugged me tightly and, kissing his face and his poor eyes, I told him where I had been, and how I had found my family, and become an independent lady. I told him I had thought I heard him calling, and come back to find him, and that I knew all about the fire.

"I have longed for you Jane," he said. "And now I can marry you, if you will have me. But how could you want me, when I am so hideous, and you are a wealthy lady, who can have whatever she pleases?"

"It is you I want," I said. "You are what pleases me.

And anyway, you were not handsome before. I told you that once, remember?"

He laughed. "Then, Jane, will you marry me?"

Reader, I married him. We have been married for ten years now – the happiest years of my life. We live at Fearndean, with John and Mary, and Adele is at school nearby. And we have two children of our own.

Two years after we were married, Edward was dictating a letter to me, when suddenly he leaned forward and said: "Jane, are you wearing a blue dress? And do you have a golden pendant around your neck?"

One of his eyes had started to work again, just a little. We went to London to visit an eye doctor, and Edward regained his sight in that eye just enough to see his way, so that he no longer had to be led by the hand. And when his first-born child was put into his arms, he could look at his little son, and see how he resembled him.

Mary and Diana were married too – Diana to a navy captain, and Mary to a vicar. They are both happy, and we visit each other often.

And as for St. John – he went to India alone after all. He wrote to us all a year later, saying that he was suffering from a fever, and thought that God might call him to Heaven soon. After that, we never heard from him again.

Glossary

This glossary explains words and phrases used in *Jane Eyre* that may be unfamiliar to modern readers.

apothecary An old word for a pharmacist or chemist, or anyone who makes and sells medicines.

benefactress A female benefactor – someone who provides money as a form of charity.

chilblains Painful, itchy swellings on the hands and feet, caused by extreme cold.

consumption Another name for tuberculosis or TB, a serious disease that can affect the lungs.

hamlet A tiny village.

footman A male servant who wears a uniform and greets people at the front door, or travels with them in a carriage.

missionary Someone who travels abroad to try to convert other people to a particular religion, especially Christianity.

porter's lodge A small house at the gateway of a castle, mansion, or other large building.

stroke Illness caused by a blockage in the brain.

typhus An infectious disease spread by by fleas, lice or mites. It causes a high fever and can be fatal.

vicar A priest of the Church of England.

Movies

Since film was invented at the end of the 19th century, *Jane Eyre* has been adapted for the screen at least seven times, as well as being made into a stage play and an opera. The first film version, starring Virginia Bruce, was made in 1934, and ten years later another *Jane Eyre* was filmed, starring Joan Fontaine as Jane and the great film star Orson Welles as Rochester. Many film buffs still think these classic early versions are the best.

However, two modern adaptations, made in 1996 and 1997, are also very popular. The first, directed by Franco Zeffirelli (who is famous for other literary adaptations, including *Romeo and Juliet* and *Hamlet*), stars French actress Charlotte Gainsbourg as Jane, and William Hurt as Rochester. It was filmed in the north of England and in Italy, and is full of lush photography and beautiful romantic landscapes.

The 1997 movie, made for television, features British actors Samantha Morton and Ciaran Hinds. It is shorter and less extravagant than Zeffirelli's film, but some fans feel it is the one that best captures the passionate spark between Rochester and Jane.